A William's Hunt
Steampunk Time Pirates Novel

By
Krista Cagg

The Milan Job

For information contact :
http://www.tamingchaos.net/krista-cagg
Interior and cover design by Chaos Publications

ISBN: 9 7 8 1 9 5 4 4 1 3 1 4 6
1st Edition: July 2023

Acknowledgements

There are far too many people to thank for their encouragement, support and contributions to what went into making this series, but I can't get away with simply saying "you know who you are". I would like to point out that this list is in no particular order, other than my mind spewed your name out randomly. So without further delay, I would like to thank the following for being incredibly awesome:

My parents: Barb, Jack, Lois and Ed. All of them have encouraged the weird in me.

Jen: For not letting me give up and being the best bestie ever.

Midnight Syndicate: Ed! You started it all by encouraging me to write that novelette! It will see print some day!

This Way to the Egress: For being some awesome sounds on the playlist, and muses in your own right!

Frenchy and the Punk: More "must haves" on the playlist!

Jana Oliver: For saying just the "write" thing at just the right time when you really didn't have to.

Steam on, my friends!

Forward

I read an article recently that stated that a corporation in a major metropolitan area was offering its employees a fifteen percent raise if they got a tattoo of the company's logo. Fifteen percent! And the only qualification the employee needed to have was a blank canvas of skin to be emblazoned with a corporation's insignia (on their own nickel) for all time. They didn't own shares in the company. They had nothing to do with the formation of the business. They didn't even have to put in a certain amount of time dedicated to the betterment of the corporation's investments. They just had to be willing to be branded.

Think about that for a minute then ask yourself a few questions. Do you care enough about the machine you work for that you would be willing to mark yourself permanently? Are you tempted enough by a cash reward that you would make yourself a walking billboard? Don't we give enough of ourselves to our jobs on the hope that maybe this year we might see a few more dollars added to our salary? Have we fallen from dignity so far that it is snicker-worthy that people are having to do whatever it takes to earn a decent wage, including that they sacrifice the only thing they truly own?

Don't get me wrong. I'm not against tattoos. I have three myself but they are three very personal tattoos that have nothing to do with a money-making powerhouse that cuts me a check so I can live. I don't even have ink reflective of these books.

So what about these books? Am I suggesting that they have an anti-corporation theme? To a certain degree. I have to admit that much. But they are more about the potential to take greed and power to a place that is categorically…wrong. Greed by itself is ugly, but can be impotent. Power by itself can lean to either moral polarity. Combine the two and then give it some nifty new technology and you have the recipe for a cocktail of corruption. We humans have seen it before. Seen it and stood up to it. Sometimes we failed horribly and the corruption spread, but sometimes, when those strong few ground in and shouted to the gale "no more!" change stopped the corruption in its tracks.

To understand where the crew of *The William's Hunt* is coming from you have to understand their captain, Captain Alexandria de Sade. Imagine working hard to gain the achievements and advancements you have doing groundbreaking work in a new field that promised mankind phenomenal insight to its own origins. You had a front row seat for putting together pieces of the puzzle that would explain why we got to where we are. You got to physically touch people, places and things that made our growth possible. And you believed entirely in the conglomeration that put you there. Until one day you had the curtains pulled back, and saw that the shine was a hologram. The little man at the controls had strings attached to his wrists and mouth, but you couldn't see the hands that manipulated them. You learned that the only reason that the powers-that-be do what they do was to line their pockets and worse. Wouldn't that be a heart shattering feeling of betrayal?

So what can you do? Now that you know the truth. Options are varied. Some safe. Some, not so much. But if you are like Captain Alex, they would be the right thing to do even if that meant you sacrificed all of the accomplishments you had worked for. The fabled Robin Hood did this. We see it a lot in modern day pop culture and entertainment, but it is founded on some very real historical happenings. Such a comparison is not lost on a captain of a time machine, and Captain Alex is more than willing to skew her moral compass towards piracy in order to see the right thing done. And she brought a handful of characters along for the ride.

So, avast! Splice the main brace, and sit before the mast while you read the accounts of Captain Alex and the crew of *The William's Hunt* as they set about exposing the nefarious deeds of the corrupt corporation Naviwerks! Might be that you'll be reminded that no King or country or corporation defines who you are, but your deeds and your will to stand for what you believe in.

"I have more respect for somebody who points at his ideal - in this case, the ideal of the pirate - and then becomes something that's more radical, more exciting, more subversive than a pirate could ever be."
–Will Oldham

The Crew

Captain Alexandria de Sade: Former Captain of Naviwerks gone pirate, now Captain of the stolen chrono-ship *The William's Hunt*

Laurence Kane: Formerly hopelessly unemployed, now Horotech for Captain de Sade.

Gerard "Geri" Reynolds: Former member of the Naviwerks Security Corp, now Security Officer for Captain de Sade.

Angelica "Angel" Flynn: Once a Pilot for commercial transport, now Pilot for Captain de Sade

Nigel Wellington III: Former Historian of Naviwerks, now Historian for Captain de Sade.

Dr. Abraham Hennessey: Formerly retired physician, now Ship's Doctor for Captain de Sade.

1. **ho·rol·o·gy**/həˈräləjē/

Noun: a. The study and measurement of time.
b. The art of making clocks and watches.

Shove Off

I
Welcome Aboard, Mr. Kane

Laurence Kane stood alone on the dock in his best suit, a three-piece affair of a faded mocha color complete with matching bowler. Rather, it would have matched if it had seen as much of the sun as the suit itself had. That not being the case, it was more the original color than the coat, vest and pants. His bland brown hair had been recently trimmed to above his collar, curling at the ends where they poked out from beneath his hat.

Two worn, leather cases sat side by side on his left. The smaller valise contained his personal effects and all of his clothing. The larger case was in better condition than the one beside it. It received more attention and care than its fellow, since it contained his precious instruments and tools, some of which were of his own design. Binders, winders, widgets, gears, and cogs. Vials of chemicals in liquid or solid form and vacuum-sealed tubes of gases. Books on the subject of Horology, some on the movement of time and the perception thereof, and some on clock making techniques and repair. Books on the history of the chrono-engines. And the collection of his own, unpublished, hand-written notebooks on Horotechnology that contained, according to his professors, some of the most ridiculous yet genius approaches to the science of time travel and the machinery that made it possible. In short, it was the basic kit every good horotech required when reporting for duty.

Glancing about, he removed his worn and scuffed pocket watch from the breast pocket of his vest to check the time. It was absolutely correct, of course. He was on time. Actually, it was a few minutes past the time he was to have met a representative from his new assignment. Laurence let out a quiet sigh as he tucked the watch back into the pocket, and looked at his surroundings then muttered under his breath. "…dock seventeen, warehouse five…" He was where he was supposed to be, but remained alone. No liaison. *Perhaps*, he thought, *they had found another horotech and my services are no longer required.* That would be catastrophic since prior attempts had proven that his ability to obtain a respectable position in his field of study was even worse than his ability to maintain employment of even the humblest kind. The only thing he did seem to be proficient at in his short time as a working member of society was his innate ability to get himself sacked.

"Get yourself together, man," Laurence advised himself as he tugged on the hem of his suit coat in a futile attempt to straighten out the creases. "She assured you that they weren't interested in anyone but you for their engines." He didn't sound as certain as he strived to be. He always appeared to be nervous and worried, but his expression became more so as his mind replayed his interview with Captain de Sade.

"...assure you, madam, that-"

"Captain."

"I beg your pardon?"

"Captain, Mr. Kane."

Laurence couldn't recall seeing eyes so pale or coldly blue, let alone having them regard him with such intensity. Even her voice seemed to hold a chilly edge to it as she corrected his form of address. "I hold a rank for a reason, even if it isn't officially recognized. I expect members of my crew to respect that."

Laurence had gone a bit gape-mouthed not for the minor chastisement, but for the surprise of being numbered amongst her crew. Or was he being presumptuous? No, she had made it perfectly clear that she expected him to hold to a certain mode of behavior as befitted her subordinate. He blinked. "Does...does this mean that I am hired?" He shifted in his chair as he stammered. "Captain...I mean."

The way her lips curved and made her expression sly and knowing didn't comfort him. Laurence knew he wasn't an aggressive man by any stretch of the imagination, but that didn't mean he enjoyed being mocked by the fairer sex any better than a wharf soldier might. "Mr. Kane you were hired from the moment I read your dossier at Naviwerks. Your talents speak for themselves." Her lips twitched again with amusement. "Regardless of your employment history. I believe you will be a most welcome addition to The William."

Then she had given him a packet of information that contained a time and location for him to report to duty as well as a very brief job description, a fact he would only find out later that night when he sat down to examine the contents more thoroughly. "Follow the instructions in the packet closely, Mr. Kane. Deviate from them in any way or follow through on the temptation to interpret them creatively and you will find yourself left six days behind me."

It was a devilish threat, and one that Laurence took to heart. He felt somewhat dumbfounded as she stood up and left the dodgy public house in which they had met without another word.

Laurence pressed his lips together as he looked around again for any sign of someone. Well, someone who didn't belong in this dismal location. He was fairly certain he wouldn't enjoy an encounter with an employee of the docks or worse, a member of Harbor Security. Since he did not possess the ability to lie believably, he did not want to be asked about his business around the dockside warehouses. Somehow he doubted *reporting for duty aboard a chrono-ship gone pirate* would be received genially by those in authority.

"Ah, Mr. Kane." Laurence nearly leaped out of his scuffed shoes in surprise at the voice that chimed out lyrically behind him. He whirled around to see a handsome man leaning against the warehouse door, the entrance door. The Horotech blinked in astonishment. It was a perpetual state of mind for Laurence.

The tall man sauntered towards him with a jaunty set to his lips. "Right on time." The man seemed to find that amusing if the chuckle that came from him were any indication.

Laurence collected himself as best he could as he nudged his spectacles higher on the bridge of his nose with a finger scarred and calloused from his work with the machines he loved so well. "Not to put too fine a point on it, sir, but I was on time several minutes ago." He cleared his throat and blushed as he realized too late that he might have come across as belligerent and insubordinate, never minding that time was precisely why he had been hired.

A bright and charming smile broke across the man's face just before he laughed. After stopping next to Laurence, the man clapped him on the shoulder. "Well said, man! Well said."

He continued to grin even as Laurence winced at the familiarity that the man showed him. The hand remained on Laurence's shoulder, a fact which made the shorter man uncomfortable, but he wasn't forward enough to ask the man to remove it.

"My name is Nigel Wellington the Third. Ship's Historian. I anticipate we will be working closely with one another." Mr. Wellington slid his hand down Laurence's arm, a gesture that caused the Horotech to shiver a little, and then held it at waist level in proffered greeting.

What choice did Laurence have? Something about this Mr. Wellington put him on edge even more than others did, but if what was said were true then Laurence would indeed work often with him. It wouldn't do to alienate the man just because Laurence wasn't socially adjusted. Awkwardly, he shook the

Historian's hand, but kept it as brief as possible. "Ah… indeed." His smile was just as awkward as his reply, but Mr. Wellington didn't seem to mind. In fact, he appeared to be even more amused. "A task I'm sure will be both a pleasure and a challenge."

"A pleasure, indeed." Nigel scanned the Horotech over. Laurence flushed again, and cleared his throat under the man's scrutiny. The action seemed to only encourage the Historian, but a moment later Wellington chuckled and took a step back, relinquishing his claim on Laurence's personal space. "Best we hurry on, then. The Captain is not a patient woman." Wellington looked to the cases beside Laurence and sighed. But then he smiled at Laurence before he made for the warehouse door. "Come along, Mr. Kane. Leave your bags."

Laurence blinked some more, looked to his cases then to Mr. Wellington's back. *Leave* his precious case? The man was mad! "B-but, Mr. Wellington…" He lifted a hand in weak protest since his voice wouldn't rise to the occasion. "…I'm afraid I really must insist against that. You see ah-"Laurence's complaint trailed off when he took notice that Mr. Wellington wasn't walking any further than the entrance door to the warehouse they were standing before. The Historian didn't even glance over his shoulder as he pulled open the door and stepped in. Laurence made the conscious effort to shut his lips then followed. What he found within was not what he had expected.

He stepped over the threshold into the warehouse, but Laurence wasn't as graceful as the ship's Historian. He caught the toe of his shoe and stumbled, but paid it no mind, as his attention was enraptured with the sight before him. From the outside he never would have credited the warehouse to have the space to fit what was contained within, but some clever person had hollowed out the walls to the units on either side of warehouse five, and sank the flooring, as well. Laurence's hands gripped the cool metal railing that ran along the catwalk he had tripped onto and he stared in awe at what he had found. "….my God! She's beautiful."

The chrono-ship *The William's Hunt* nested in her moorings as comfortably as a knife in a sheath. The hull was the standard alloy used to withstand the transit through time, crafted so that the visual end result was somewhere between the greenish hints of bronze and the high shine of brass, accented in frames that had touches of chrome. In the darkness she was lovely. In the light of day she would rival the sun.

Although not intended for extended flight, chrono-ships were capable of it. Based on what Laurence saw in the pockmarks and scuffs on the nose and belly of the ship, Captain de Sade did make use of the ability. Not that there appeared to be any neglect. Some captains saw such wear and tear as battle scars to be proud of, but the worst on *The William's Hunt* had been buffed and polished. Laurence's quick eyes picked out the details that told him that Captain de Sade allowed for some wear on the ship. However it was just as obvious that she insisted on a high quality of maintenance. He felt a smile pull at his lips and a huff of astonishment pass through them as he realized that he was already under the ship's spell. "Fantastic!"

"Any problems, Wellington?" A deep voice that seemed edged with sharp gravel rumbled up from the moorings a good fifty feet beneath the catwalk. Laurence tore his attention from the chrono-ship to the source of that intimidating voice. It belonged to a man that even from that distance the Horotech could tell would tower over him. It wasn't just what he would call an unnatural height, but the man had shoulders made for building pyramids or transporting small villages from one place to another, and had arms to match. And he was eyeing Laurence as if he were uncertain if what he was looking at was human.

"None at all," Nigel replied as he descended the ladder from the catwalk to the floor below. His rakish smile was turned up toward Laurence as he answered the roughneck.

Laurence was positive he would never be on quite that easy of terms with either man, and for a moment he wondered just what he had gotten himself into.

As if a mind reader, Nigel shot the Horotech a wink. "You might see to his bags though, Geri. Doubtful anyone else will get them down the ladder." He turned a blithe smile to the brick of a man who glowered in return. The Historian paid it no mind as he called back up to Laurence, who was dithering in indecision. "Come on, Mr. Kane! Let's get you out of our good Mr. Reynolds way. Unpleasant at the best of times, he becomes downright surly when he has to trip all over people."

"Right." Laurence's reply was more to himself than an acknowledgment to Mr. Wellington. It seemed to be the trigger that got him detached from the railing, and he moved to the ladder. His concern for his bags was diminished in direct proportion to his fascination for the ship he was soon to board.

Laurence's descent was less graceful and quick than Mr. Wellington's, and was closely observed by the ship's Security Officer, Gerard "Geri" Reynolds. His arms crossed over his expansive chest, he frowned as he spoke to Nigel in a low undertone. "Here's hoping the Captain's little project is better at navigating a chrono-engine than he is a stinkin' ladder." Nigel laughed quietly as he leaned against one of the hydraulic bars of the ramp to the ship's hold. His eyes glittered with amusement and excitement. "She didn't hire him for his agility on the monkey bars." A smirk plucked at his lips as his fingers laced themselves together loosely before his mid-section. "Give him a chance in the engine room. If he doesn't live up to the Captain's expectations, then I dare say our first port of call will be his final departure."

Laurence finished his descent and stumbled backward away from the ladder. His head was craned back so he could look back up to the catwalk. A quiet sound of astonishment huffed out of him as he felt a little lightheaded. It would have been impossible for him to have brought his cases down with him.

He was startled out of his reverie when a large hand gripped his shoulder and the smell of sweat invaded his senses. Laurence turned to find himself face to chest with Mr. Reynolds. He raised his eyes to the brute, who pressed his lips together into a disapproving line before he gave the Horotech a push toward Mr. Wellington. Turning, the man proceeded to practically fly up the ladder to the catwalk. Laurence shuffled towards the Historian and felt more than a little intimidated and overwhelmed. *Honestly! The man was a gorilla!* Laurence huffed to himself.

Laurence turned to Mr. Wellington with an apologetic and weak smile on his face. “I’m afraid I am not making a very good first impression. I admit I get on better with machines than I do people, so I promise you a ride in the ship to be smoother than a conversation with me.”

Nigel lifted from his lazy lean as he gave a friendly sound of amusement to his newest fellow crew member. He guided Laurence to the ramp with a casual touch of his hand to his shoulder. “Never fear, Mr. Kane.” He smiled down to the little man. “Geri openly despises everyone with equal measure, save the Captain. If he does suddenly seem to like you *then* you need to start worrying and sleep with one eye open.”

Laurence was not reassured.

The two entered *The William’s Hunt* via her hold. Crates, barrels, shelves, chests and various other storage units were arranged strategically throughout the belly of the ship in a manner that allowed for space to hold cargo with maximum efficiency. Everything was anchored by ripstop cord nets, chains or braided metal. One entire wall of the hold was lined with unadorned oaken wardrobes that contained era after era of garb and accessories. They were staples for any retrieval team.

Laurence deduced their purpose immediately when he saw them. If each wardrobe signified an era, then the Captain and her crew were prepared for almost every fashion need. Obviously, Captain de Sade made off with more than just a chrono-ship when she left Naviwerks' employment. Laurence felt himself grow more impressed with the Captain and her temerity, but a nugget of apprehension took root as well. *The corporation would be put out by the loss of the ship and their best captain, but to have lost goods and God knew what else...?* Certain truths were beginning to take root in Laurence's mind. *This pirating business is becoming a very real prospect, complete with all of the excitement and danger.*

"This, of course, is the hold." Nigel looked somewhat disdainfully at their surroundings and gestured to the contents with an idle flap of his hand. "Nothing you and I need concern ourselves with. This tends to be the domain of Mr. Reynolds. He catalogs the inventory daily, I believe, so there will never be a worry about supplies, thank God."

'Thank Mr. Reynolds' would be more appropriate, thought Laurence, but he wasn't so bold as to say so out loud. He didn't understand Mr. Wellington's attitude towards the hold. The man looked as if he smelled something foul, perhaps as if he were giving Laurence a tour of a middens instead of a ship's hold. What did he expect would be here? Not that Laurence had much time to contemplate the matter since his guide moved them along to a lift in the far corner as quickly as possible.

Nigel let Laurence enter the lift first, and then pulled the dulled brass lattice gate shut after he stepped inside. The Horotech took notice of the Historian's well-manicured hand as it wrapped around the lever. His spider-like fingers depressed the grip before they deftly pushed the rod forward to activate the mechanism. Mr. Wellington was obviously a man of means. Not a callus or hangnail was to be seen, but it was the signet ring on his right middle finger that told Laurence of the man's family wealth. The stylized 'W' was a dead giveaway. Laurence wondered which Wellington family Nigel was attached to.

They began to rise and soon the hold disappeared. There was nothing clunky or jerky about the lift's movement. Laurence was again impressed with the condition in which their Captain kept her ship. It allowed his mind to drift towards his cases, and he hoped that Mr. Reynolds had retrieved them from outside the warehouse before someone had made off with them. It occurred to him a moment later that even if they had gone missing they were in a chrono-ship. All they needed to do to reclaim his effects would be to slip back to the moment he had entered the warehouse. Simple, really.

He was brought out of his musings by the lift coming to a stop. Nigel replaced the lever into the neutral position before he threw open the lattice gate. "Here we are." He gestured for Laurence to precede him out of the lift. A more genial smile returned to his face. "After you Mr. Kane."

Laurence returned the smile with a little more ease as he stepped out of the lift. The excitement of a new assignment overrode any discomfort he felt at the prospect of meeting new people. He looked around the passageway in which he found himself, and admired the mahogany wainscoting with its thin brass detailing that accented the dark reddish wood. The dark tones were offset by soft rose-colored wallpaper above with scrolling gold and black leaf trim that ran parallel to the ceiling. Every five feet or so was a swath of fabric of a rich forest green damask that was gathered tightly and anchored into the wainscoting. Brass sconces were affixed at the curtains. Their electric lights flickered to give the illusion of gas flames. Their light was enough to see by but not so bright as to ruin the atmosphere that was created. All in all, it made for a quite warm and welcoming feel to the interior, one that Laurence approved.

An elderly and somewhat portly man bustled around the corner at an intersection in the passageway ahead of Laurence. The Horotech was surprised when he was only given a cursory grimace by the man who then proceeded to look past him to Mr. Wellington. In his hand he held an illuminated note panel, the other hand wiggled the stylus between his fingers. A gruff smile forced its way onto his lips as he stopped next to Laurence, but still seemed to give him no notice.

"Nigel." He spoke the Historian's name as if he stated a fact that indeed, his name was Nigel, and the elderly man was well aware of that. "Tell me Reynolds filled the list I gave him." He shook his head, which made his jowls jiggle and animated the well-trimmed mutton chop whiskers that were practically white with age. "We will not be leaving without the list being completed otherwise. I told her over and over."

Nigel put an amiable smile on his face as he held up a slender hand in a pacifying gesture. "Why ask me? I fulfilled my pre-flight task by bringing aboard the newest member of our crew of ill repute." His amused chuckle was a bit muted by the close quarters of the passageway, and he gestured towards Laurence as he joined him. "Meet Mr. Laurence Kane. Our new Horotech." His brows lifted expectantly. "Mr. Kane, Dr. Hennessey. Our ship's doctor."

Laurence extended his hand. His enthusiasm made him bolder. "How do you—"

He was interrupted by the doctor's harrumph. Dr. Hennessey neither shook his hand, nor gave him anything more than a brief scan before he looked back to Nigel. "Safe to assume that he is in the hold going over strappings that he knows damned well will stay put since he just set them himself not ten minutes ago for the fifth time."

"Of course." Nigel's smile was the definition of patience for the doctor's mannerisms.

Dr. Hennessey harrumphed again then turned his attention to Laurence, finally. He looked the little Horotech up and down then started towards the lift Laurence and Mr. Wellington had just exited. "Eat some spinach, young man. Get some iron into your system. You're simply pallid." The passing diagnosis was given in a grumbling undertone as the doctor went back to his note panel, and tapped the glowing screen with the stylus.

Laurence was back to feeling as if he weren't going to make an impression other than bad on any of the crew. Mr. Wellington seemed to get on with everyone he came across so perhaps there was that, even though something about the man's behavior made Laurence uncomfortable to have him in close proximity. For instance, the Historian again placed his hand on

Laurence's shoulder to get him moving. *Must the man be so entirely tactile?*

"Soon enough you'll be as jaded as the rest of us if only from exposure," Nigel said in a blithe tone. His amused smirk seemed a perpetual fixture upon his face. His hand didn't linger on Laurence's shoulder for long. When they reached the intersection he gestured down first one hall then the other. "Down there is medical and Dr. Hennessey's quarters. My own lay down that hall along with my modest library. Continuing down this direction are guest quarters, not that we expect to have many. We aren't exactly giving tours." His lips tightened into a more lopsided, amused cant. He continued straight on to where a set of metal stairs led up from the deck.

"Above will be the mess hall," Nigel made a face, "not a very appealing term, but when in Rome…"

The Historian's opinion of the term was proven inappropriate. After they climbed the switch back staircase the pair stepped into a dining hall suitable for nobility at the very least. Laurence stared in astonishment. He marveled at the cherry wood cabinets, polished granite surfaces, clean gas range and oven. Pots, pans, goblets of pewter and wood hung from pegs that descended from the ceiling or hung on the walls. One could assume that the plates and dinnerware were contained within the cabinets and drawers that all had shiny brass fixtures. The common table was made of the same cherry wood, as were the benches on either side. The heads of the table hosted chairs, but Laurence noted that instead of plush velvet padding the chairs were modest, polished wood and nothing else. He had assumed that the Captain would allow herself that level of luxury, or perhaps Naviwerks would since *The William's Hunt* had been decorated and designed by the corporation. Laurence surmised either such accommodations were reserved elsewhere for the captain of the ship, or Captain de Sade had no use for such fripperies.

"With the exception of evenings you attend to your own meals." Nigel moved through the mess hall toward the doorway on the other end of the long room without lingering. Laurence was forced to hurry to catch up with his guide. "Dr. Hennessey has a liking for preparing dinner, but he steadfastly refuses to cook any other meal. Can't understand why." Nigel made a quiet sound of amusement for that. "The Captain doesn't see the need to hire a cook full on so I do hope you know how to at least boil water." It was obvious that there was some sort of inside joke there.

"No, that won't be a problem," assured Laurence as he caught up to Mr. Wellington's back just as the Historian began to climb a short flight of steps. "You see I'm an only child and my mother was quite ill most of my life before she passed, rest her soul. I was forced to learn to cook for myself at a young age."

Nigel glanced back at Mr. Kane with a brow lifted. "I see." He seemed to ponder the Horotech for a moment before his lips pulled into a nebulous smile. Then he turned to push open a hatch door. "My sympathies, Mr. Kane. For your mother." There was something tight, almost restrained about his tone of voice. Since he had been nothing but glib thus far the tone was notable."I loved my own dearly." But before that could be commented on, Nigel moved into the passageway past the hatch. Laurence thought it a curious thing to say, but for once managed to pick up on the social nuances that meant Mr. Wellington didn't wish to discuss the topic.

The passageway they stepped into was much the same as the one beneath, although the lighting seemed a tad dimmer to Laurence's eyes. It was shorter, with a set of metal stairs that led upward on either end. The first was immediately to the left as they entered from the mess hall, the other on the far end just past an intersection. Perhaps the darkened lighting was meant to set the tone for the Horotech's next encounter, for there, at the base of the far staircase, stood the Captain herself.

Even from where he stood, Laurence could feel those impossibly pale blue eyes trained on him as if they were capable of seeing straight into his thoughts. The coldness within them seemed to affect his blood. It ran with a chill that raised gooseflesh on the back of his neck. The set of her lips, which held the color of fine burgundy wine, did nothing to reassure him of her fair reception of him to her boat. Her gentle waves of auburn hair were pinned behind her head and allowed to cascade down her back. Everything about her was beautiful, but her presence was so commanding that one tended to overlook the fact that she was so petite, so slight. No woman that Laurence had seen managed to make a pair of flared thigh military jodhpurs and spotless black jack boots look so elegant. Granted, the tight, light beige cotton tank she wore under a pair of suspenders that held her gun belt in place might have helped bring forth her feminine appeal. Her slender, delicate fingers drummed idly against the simple silver hilt of a rapier on the hip opposite the one that bore the holster that contained her plasma pistol. Laurence just knew his heart and breathing had stopped at the sight of her, but more from fear than from appreciation of Captain de Sade's loveliness.

"Ah, my dear Captain!" To Laurence's horror Nigel strode right up to the woman without a care. Worse, he lifted her hand when he reached her then placed a sweet kiss to her dainty knuckles. Laurence expected the woman to draw her rapier and run Mr. Wellington through, or to at least pull her pistol and shoot him in the foot for his bold familiarity. Instead, all she did was roll her eyes with a long suffering sigh. "As always a pleasure to lay eyes on your visage."

Captain de Sade pulled her hand out from Nigel's grip then flapped it at him in a graceful if dismissive gesture, her lips pressed together. "Don't be tiresome, Nigel." Her voice was a silken alto that sounded capable of achieving volumes that could range from a sultry whisper to a commanding shout. Laurence decided that never before had a ship and her captain been so well paired.

The Horotech mustered up some courage, enough to approach the pair with a slight clearing of his throat and a strained smile that he tried to make look more confident than it was. He at least would be able to say later that he didn't flinch when the Captain turned her attention to him instead of on Mr. Wellington. The smile she gave him held little warmth, but that might have been the influence of her eyes.

"Hello, Captain de Sade." Laurence's voice wavered only slightly as he greeted her. He adopted what he hoped was a smart stance, his hands clasped behind his back, mostly so she wouldn't notice that they were shaking. "I am reporting for duty, and may I say that I am enthusiastically looking forward to serving on such a splendid craft?" *There. That wasn't too bad. Was it?* It was difficult to tell by the Captain's reaction.

"No less than I expected, Mr. Kane," she replied in a flat tone of voice. Whatever thoughts she had on her Horotech were hidden behind a well-controlled expression of cool disdain. Silence then lingered between them as if she waited for him to do something interesting.

Laurence fought against the urge to fidget in place and lowered his eyes before he belatedly remembered to remove his hat in the presence of a lady. He fumbled the bowler from his head, but was grateful that it gave his hands something to hold on to. "Ah…as directed, I read through my hiring packet, but…if you please…my job description was somewhat lacking in details. Perhaps…at your convenience…we could discuss it. You and I." He swallowed as the Captain arched a delicate brow. "Over tea." Both he and the Captain ignored the quiet titter that was barely contained by Mr. Wellington.

"The details I gave you are no more and no less than what I had intended to give you, Mr. Kane." Captain de Sade's chin came up into a more prideful cant. Her smile didn't seem to warm, but there was an edge of amusement to it that made her seem more human. "I expect you to fill in the blanks since you would know better than I what tasks are required of a Horotech. Any lack in your performance will be brought to light in time and remedied immediately."

Laurence blinked in open bewilderment. Never before had he encountered an employment where *he* was responsible for writing his own job description as well as hold himself to standards. Always he knew some form of management would look over his shoulder, place expectations on his performance that may or may not have anything to do with his actual work. Apparently, the same assumptions applied to Captain de Sade was a mistake. Additionally, he began to get the impression that one would be wise to not try to anticipate how the Captain's mind worked. That was both reassuring and daunting.

"Y-yes, ma-" Laurence broke off his words as a blush came to his cheeks. She arched a brow at him again. "Captain. I mean. Yes, Captain," he stammered.

Nigel studied his fingernails until Captain de Sade spoke. "Take him to his quarters, Mr. Wellington."

Her eyes never left the Horotech as she began to turn to ascend the stairs. Laurence felt himself begin to breathe again just in time for her to pause in her steps. "Oh and," this time she waited until Laurence looked at her, "welcome aboard, Mr. Kane." Her lips melted into a tight smile before she turned completely to climb the stairs.

Nigel watched their Captain stride up the stairs then draped a companionable arm around Laurence's shoulders. He encouraged the Horotech to start back towards the stairs by the entrance to the mess hall. His voice lowered to a husky undertone that was colored by open amusement. "Butter wouldn't melt in the good Captain's mouth, but she has an ass you could bounce a coin off of."

"My God, man!" Laurence's outrage at their Captain described in such disrespectful words overrode his withdrawn nature. He skewered Mr. Wellington with a scowl of disapproval as he pulled out from under the Historian's arm. To his continued consternation, all his protest seemed to do was amuse Mr. Wellington because the Historian started to laugh with a pleased grin on his face.

"Do calm down, Mr. Kane," said Nigel around his mirth. He gave Laurence's arm a gentle prod to keep him moving. "I've said much worse to her face, and the fact that it has the benefit of being true is what keeps me in her good graces."

The man is insane! How Nigel maintained his position as ship's historian, regardless of how clever, accurate and thorough he might be with his research, was beyond Laurence's comprehension. He would never presume to say such a thing about any woman let alone one that held his livelihood in her hands. Her rank and accomplishments commanded the very least of respect. Other men might take Mr. Wellington to task, take up the lady's cause and defend her honor in a time proven manner. Unfortunately, Laurence knew exactly what the end result would be should he choose to deliver such a challenge. The women of the world must search for a champion outside of him, but that didn't stop him from delivering a scathing look.

Nevertheless, Laurence knew he couldn't estrange Mr. Wellington. They would work closely together, and it made no sense to create a hostile work environment for himself by picking a battle he honestly had no right to involve himself in. Captain de Sade was a clever woman who seemed to know her crew. He put forth an effort to contain his affront.

"Indeed." Laurence smoothed his hands over the lapels of his suit coat then gave an indignant sniff before he let the subject go. He continued to walk with Mr. Wellington instead without the need to be encouraged along. "Now if you please, I'd like to see the engines and my quarters."

Nigel's pleased grin remained on his face as he inclined his head towards Mr. Kane. "Yes, of course. Fortunately for you they are one and the same." He gestured for Laurence to climb the stairs before him.

If Laurence had been impressed by what he had thus far seen of *The William's Hunt,* he was downright overcome by what he found in her engine room. This was to be his little world, his kingdom, since here *his* word was law by the Captain's say so. He had expected to see something marginal that he could improve upon as he gained time, equipment and parts. What waited for him was quite the opposite. Laurence found himself gazing adoringly upon what was, in his opinion, the most beautiful part of the entire ship, and his outrage at the Historian's cheek was forgotten.

The engine was in two parts. The back two thirds were the turbine that propelled the ship in flight. It was the least of Laurence's interest since any monkey that understood mechanics could operate, repair and maintain that part. The front third was what concerned him, as that was the chrono-engine itself. The same alloys that made up the hull of the ship encased the engine, as well as made up the framing that contained the thick glass polymer where all of the magic happened. A certain arrangement of atoms, when charged up by a certain measure of static and then flooded with steam created by a combination of heated liquids, punched a hole through reality into the past. In other words: it created a wormhole. Once through the wormhole the engines would recognize the chrono-pattern for the entry way for five days. Within that time, the engines could reopen the hole and reverse the transfer to return the ship to the point in time from which it came. But if the window of opportunity was missed they would be stranded in the past until another ship towed them back through another wormhole. This made marauding, pirating, and other mercenary work, outside of Naviwerks, dangerous and risky ventures since there would not be a friendly fleet to retrieve them.

Laurence had seen and worked with chrono-engines in his university days when he earned his Horotechnology degree, but they had been earlier, less desirable designs. They were good for students to tinker with and learn from, but not for current, commercial use. He had seen diagrams for the chrono-engines in present use by Naviwerks, and all hope of using and working on one rested upon being hired by the corporation that held a monopoly on time travel, a task he had never managed to accomplish. That is until Captain de Sade approached him and made her offer. As Laurence looked upon the marvelous machinery before him every hurdle he met with thus far was worth it. Laurence Kane was in love!

Nigel stood behind Mr. Kane, who seemed to be stuck on the top of the short set of stairs that led down into the engine room. He touched his hand to Laurence's shoulder and gave it a gentle nudge. "Welcome home, my good fellow." Nigel smiled to Laurence when the he glanced at him then the Horotech started down the stairs into his little kingdom. The Historian chuckled to himself then turned with a small shake of his head, intent on returning to his own quarters from which he could inform Reynolds that Mr. Kane was settled and his cases could be delivered.

II
Shove Off

Captain Alexandria de Sade stepped onto the bridge of her ship after welcoming Mr. Kane. *Nigel must like him*, she thought. Her Historian was practically floating if the glimmer in his eyes had been any indication. She could have told him any thoughts he was entertaining about the Horotech were in vain, but Nigel most likely knew that anyway. He was just having fun with it. Alex couldn't help but wonder if Mr. Kane had figured that out yet.

It was the least of her thoughts on her newest crew member, however, as she looked over the brain of *The William's Hunt* with its myriad stations, monitors of blinking lights and subtle sounds that meant that operations proceeded normally. Her Pilot, Angel, was at the helm where she ran pre-flight tests and checks that Alex could have done herself, but that was what a pilot was for. Angel was a far better pilot than Alex was, and the Captain was not above allowing people to do their jobs.

Angelica "Angel" Flynn didn't stop in her work

for more than a glance from her hazel eyes to see who had come into her sanctuary. Captain Alex registered as an acceptable presence so Angel just turned back to the systems checks she had put into motion an hour ago. Her hand smoothed back imaginary loose strands of her medium brown hair that was held back into a simple ponytail in a needless gesture. The engines might be the heart of the ship, what gave it purpose, but without a good pilot at the helm it might as well be a very expensive paperweight.

“All aboard, Cap?” Angel asked in a distracted tone of voice. Part of what made a good pilot was the ability to be a magician at multi-tasking. She might sound like she wasn’t paying attention, but the fact was that the Captain always had her ear. While Captain de Sade did let Angel have her head with the helm she would still give orders that the Pilot would have to heed. It allowed the Captain to pick up on things the Pilot might miss.

“All aboard.” As always, Alex’s voice was quiet, calm and controlled. Her strides down the short steps from the landing at the door to the bridge were just as calculated as everything else. There wasn’t a soul alive that had ever seen her lose control, throw caution to the wind, or cut loose.

Pale blue eyes scanned over the read outs with just as much attentive control as their owner approached everything else. Alex saw nothing to comment on so after she set her rapier into a customized holder that was within easy reach, she slid into the captain’s chair. It sat on a raised dais above the hardwood floor of the bridge. Here were the plush accommodations

Mr. Kane had expected in the mess hall. Alex's chair was quilted leather padding dyed a deep red. The frame was thick by necessity to encase the wires, gears and mono-filaments that allowed her to take control of the comm, the helm, and to a certain degree the engines if need be. It was all frosted black metal except for the actual control panels that were set into the arms of the chair. Teak wood that was polished and coated with thick, clear resin all but shone by itself housed the touch pads that were her controls, framed in brass that was delicately etched with scrolling ivy and grape leaves. Some captains sat in their chair during the pre-flights and followed along with their pilots. Alex only did that if requested or in the case of an emergency.

The chair wasn't the only impressive looking item in the bridge of *The William*. The helm was made of the same black metal frame, but lacked the teak and brass touches. There wasn't enough room on the surfaces for such decorations, as the controls needed to be reached without hindrance. Timing could be critical so any obstacle that made a pilot's fingers fumble even for a moment could mean the difference between a smooth landing and one that could jar the crews' teeth loose or worse. Controls were set in three sections: Heading and Flight Control, Power, and Systems Monitor/Communications.

The Pilot sat in a chair only slightly less comfortable than the Captain's. It possessed a lower back and swiveled to allow the Pilot to reach every console with ease. The whole assembly faced a wide windshield that was sectioned into thirds. Layered faceting on the edges by the frames allowed the same glass polymer used in the chrono-engine to disperse wind shear while it increased aesthetic appeal.

"So?" Angel never looked away from her consoles as she asked the nebulous question. She was perhaps one of the few people who could get away with tweaking Captain Alex. Geri lacked the sense of humor, but he also followed Captain Alex like a dedicated guard dog.

Alex arched a slender brow at her Pilot's back. The corners of her lips pulled down a little. What was Angel up to now? *"So?"* She was pretty certain she knew what Angel wanted to know, but Alex didn't feel like playing guessing games right now.

The truth was her nerves were wound a bit tight at the moment. This would be the maiden voyage for the Naviwerks' chrono-ship as *The William's Hunt*. She knew the ship was fully operational, even beyond what the corporation found acceptable. She had higher standards than they did, but she, Geri, and Angel had made more than a few modifications that would set *The William* apart. Those modifications could interfere with a great many of functions that could jeopardize the ship's first pirate flight, and that worry rested heavily upon her regardless of how many reassurances Angel and Geri had fed her after the test runs they had made. But it was her second concern that she felt Angel wanted information about, and she was rewarded for her obstinacy when Angel next spoke.

"So," Angel emphasized the simple word and glanced over her shoulder. It allowed the Captain to see her cheeky expression. "What's he like? This Mr. Kane." She turned back to her controls when a pre-flight check chimed out to indicate that all was green for that function. "All I know is the information you gave us. Which, if you don't mind my saying so, told those of us who lack even a rudimentary understanding of Horotechnology a whopping nothing on the man by way of filling a couple of pages with blathering details." She tsked and shook her head as her clever fingers locked in the finished pre-flight check. "Such a tease, Cap."

Alex didn't mind Angel's familiar ways. In fact, they rather amused her. So long as her Pilot kept such a lack of respect confined to the bridge and just between them, Alex allowed it to continue. Angel had proven that with an audience she gave her Captain as much if not more respect than anyone else. As such, Alex never felt the need to assert her authority. It also helped that the two women had known each other since before Alex was recruited by Naviwerks, back when both of them had been serving as pilots in the Nationalist Air Force. Angel was the better of the two, yet Alex had been the one that Naviwerks had wooed while Angel went on to pilot Hummingbird class ships for a small charter company that ferried goods and passengers up and down the coast.

That amusement tugged at Alex's lips. She had known that her crew wouldn't be satisfied with the information she had given them about their new Horotech. But how exactly did one describe Mr. Kane? Mousy? Timid? Those were not reassuring qualities for someone who could strand them all inside a wormhole, so she had made the decision to let the crew learn of him through the time honored tradition of personal interaction aboard ship.

She won a bet that she had placed with herself on who would be the most annoyed. Angel's curiosity was tenacious, so Alex decided she would let the Pilot off the hook a little bit, and gave her an edge over the others.

That answer to Angel's question was still forthcoming, and Alex knew that the Pilot would hound her until she got her way. Never one to avoid an uncomfortable truth, Alex sighed. Her brows lowered in irritation and a small amount of concern. "Nervous. Oblivious to subtle suggestions. Inexperienced in even the slightest manner to the role of subordinate on board a vessel, and entirely unprepared for our endeavors." Alex paused as Angel actually was shocked out of her attention to the helm to turn a stunned look to her Captain. Alex smirked a little as she leaned to the right in her chair. She put her chin on the backs of her fingers. Honestly. No confidence in her ability to pick her crew. If only they knew that they, each of them, had given her the same look Angel had turned on her now about each other. Even those who had worked with each other before held some measure of surprise, maybe especially because of that fact. Regardless, Alex had every confidence in her crew, and they needed to trust her choices.

Before Angel could question her further, Alex continued with her list of Mr. Kane's qualifications. "However, he can correctly identify a problem within a chrono-engine by sound alone even before the issue creates complications. His ability to repair or replace a part is staggering in that he has accomplished even the most delicate of maintenance in a short amount of time using crude parts as temporary replacements until he has access to the proper component. And all without having to break apart the engine which would cause further potential damage."

Angel's eyes had widened at the Captain's list of Mr. Kane's talents that had earned him the invitation to join the crew as the Horotech. Nobody could replace a single part in a chrono-engine without the need to take it apart to a certain degree. That shouldn't be possible, but the Captain didn't exaggerate or believe hearsay. She saw for herself which meant that she must have witnessed Mr. Kane do just what she described.

Alex leaned forward in her chair with her eyes locked with Angel's. The upturn of her lips held an edge of pride as if she had been the one to accomplish the miracles Mr. Kane supposedly had. "That chrono-engine down there contains modifications that Mr. Kane had designed at university. His professors said they could never work, but you and I have proven already that they do." Her smile lifted as she watched Angel swallow. Some of the things those modifications were supposed to accomplish were supposed to be impossible, such as a mid-wormhole turn. But the math that Captain Alex had shown Angel did not lie. Mr. Kane was a genius!

"Does he know that you incorporated his designs?" Angel moved past being stunned into amused. Captain de Sade would use anything and everything to its fullest capacity if it would get the job done, regardless of convention or protocol. She was notorious for that, and if she hadn't been so efficient, Naviwerks would have taken her to task long before her abrupt departure from their service.

Alex's smug expression returned as she sat back in her chair again. The movement made the leather creak."No."

Angel laughed as she shook her head then turned back to her consoles. "I want to be there when he comes at you demanding to know how and where you got your hands on his designs."

The sound of heavy work boots on the landing to the bridge alerted them both to Geri's arrival. He always seemed to prefer to wear the scowl he bore now over any other expression. His reasons for it were the only thing that changed. Alex looked to her Security Officer expectantly, which he acknowledged with a curt nod as he descended the short metal latticework staircase. "Hold is secure, Cap'n. Gangway is closed, locked and sealed. We're good to go."

"Thank you, Mr. Reynolds." Alex returned his nod then turned back to Angel. "How much longer for the pre-flight, Miss Flynn?" Some captains gave their crew the honorific of Mister regardless of gender. Alex found that insulting, and had set herself apart by referring to her female crew members as Miss. It by far was not the only habit that had singled her out amongst the ship captains within Naviwerks, but it had been one of the few she possessed that had irritated the others. The waiting list of female service members of all ranks and specialties that had wanted to be part of Captain de Sade's crew had grown lengthy as her reputation gained notoriety.

Angel did a quick glance over the consoles before she answered. "Twenty minutes, Cap."

Geri's glower deepened as he took up a lean against the row of lockers that contained the motherboards, circuits and transmitter cards that were all woven together by lengths and lengths of plasma cords. His thick arms crossed over his chest. "How long does it take to prepare the engines?" His expression was dubious.

"Thirty minutes minimum for the chrono-engine to reach optimum charge," was Alex's calm and quiet reply, but a clever glint was in her eyes. "Trust me, Mr. Reynolds. We will be airborne within twenty two minutes." Before Geri could argue she turned her attention away from her Security Officer to the consoles in the arms of her chair. "Miss Flynn, I am taking the comm."

"Aye, Cap." Angel's deft fingers tapped one of the panels to turn off primary control of the communications in the helm and switched it to the Captain. She hadn't needed to since Captain de Sade could do that herself from the captain's control panels, but it was a courtesy.

Alex restrained herself from taking a deep, steadying breath as she activated the comm controls on the arm of her chair. The information she was about to share wasn't new to any of them. She might have a few more details, but they would only confirm what her crew already suspected. It might have been her conviction that faltered, but if it were, it was not enough to stay her from her course. She had already thrown herself into deep water when it came to defying Naviwerks. Even if she didn't take the next step the corporation had enough reason to have her eliminated. Through her, her crew would face the same fate even if they never turned over those engines. She owed it to the people who had put their trust in her to see this through. That was the core of her uncertainty; she could only hope that she lived up to that expectation and kept them safe. If she could have done this on her own she would have, but that was impossible even for her. There was no hope for it. She had to put her sails to the wind.

She allowed that determination to guide her as she pressed the activation button on the comms in the sequence that put her voice over the whole ship. "Attention all hands." She was pleased to hear that her voice didn't give away her inner conflict. She judged it better to not think about it too much and plunged ahead.

"As your Captain I welcome you aboard *The William's Hunt*. Some of you know that she is a stolen vessel from the Naviwerks' fleet of chrono-ships." On the bridge Alex saw Geri and Angel exchange a small but knowing smirk since they had been there to assist the Captain in procuring the ship. "They do not name their ships but number them. I have always found this practice distasteful. The corporation found it an effective way to keep captains and crews from gaining a preference for one ship over another. But none of us are employees of the corporation any longer. In order to drive that point home I have chosen a name for our ship."

Alex knew that Nigel was most likely wearing a smug expression as he sat in his Library. This had been his contribution to the ship and her Captain. "In the heyday of piracy during the 18th century Captain Calico Jack Rackham captained a sloop named *The William*. It wasn't because of his deeds that he or the ship became famous. Within his crew were the only two female pirates of the time: Mary Read and Anne Bonny. When the ship was captured they were the only two pirates that were sober, and the last to surrender." Captain Alex paused just long enough to give Angel a nod. "I intended to honor those ladies and their determination by naming my ship after theirs."

Alex knew their fate could well be her own eventually. In fact, the odds were against her ship and crew with what they faced against Naviwerks, but uninterrupted success wasn't their main goal. As she continued she hoped her crew understood that. "But that only accounts for part of the ship's name. I added my own touch to represent what we are going to accomplish." Not "trying". She wanted to make that clear. "Most of you are aware of Naviwerks' monopoly on the antiquities trade, and their…generous…endeavors towards mankind through the use of time travel. They proclaim to be saving precious artifacts that were lost to families and museums, and they do." Her voice suddenly became hard and clipped. "But at a high cost. They charge families exorbitant prices knowing that the promises of having long lost heirlooms returned to them is temptation enough. They do the same with museums and governments, all the while growing richer and more powerful than any one business should. Through their trade they have controlled elections, manipulated diplomatic decisions and reworked political rulings. Assassinations have been committed by their say so, even if evidence was spontaneously lacking."

Naviwerks had used Captain Alex's talents for their own profiteering, and had attempted to tighten their hold on her even more just before she left their employ. Alex's outrage was bordering on fury after she had learned the truth about the company she had served with unwavering loyalty. It could be heard in the subtle shift in her tone of voice—nobody cashed in on her good name. She intended to make that point abundantly clear to them. "The truth is that all of the artifacts that they offer to retrieve have already been removed from time. Naviwerks owns warehouse upon warehouse all throughout the past and present throughout the world where they store antiques, books, documents, statues and what have you that they retrieved from history, stored, labeled and documented. They then manufacture the approach to a government, museum or family where they obtain expensive contracts to agree to retrieve the item in question from the past. They use the trade and the agreements to cover their continued travels into the past to steal, hide and store more items for their warehouses. All they need do is hand over the already acquired item they signed on for to the client. And if the family or government agency falls short of the price they had agreed to Naviwerks keeps the item in trust until the monies can be raised, but they pile on an interest to the final price calling it a Holding Fee so that it becomes impossible for the clients to meet the final price. And all the while Naviwerks is making money from a sale that is never completed."

Captain Alex knew that the crew of *The William's Hunt* felt her indignation to one degree or another, but all of them agreed with her that the greed of Naviwerks had to be stopped. That was why they had signed on to her employ with only the promise of equal shares in pay. All of them had been exposed to Naviwerks' underhanded dealings in some manner. All of them save one.

Laurence Kane had tried to obtain a position with the corporation for years, but his tendency for independent thought had not been appealing to them. Alex had read the evaluation report created by Naviwerks in conjunction with his professors. He questioned authority when it came to Horotechnology, did as he pleased just because he knew without a doubt that his way was better regardless of what others thought, and was an acknowledged genius. Their intention had been to deny his degree, and let him slip into obscurity. Someone missed a memo and Laurence had graduated somewhere in the middle of his class. He was overlooked and did indeed slide into the cracks of society, but Alex had found him. She offered him the chance to prove himself.

"So what can be done?"Alex continued over the comm. "What can one small crew on a single chrono-ship do to defy a corporation the size and power of Naviwerks?" On the bridge she ceased to look at Geri and Angel. Her attention seemed to be on nothing in particular, but in her mind's eye she was seeing each member of her crew. She knew them. Trusted them. She had recruited them with an eye for their personalities as well as their unique approaches to their jobs. For this she would need a crew who could think on their feet, adapt to unusual protocols and techniques, and flourish in the face of danger. She knew that all of them were capable of shining through, even Mr. Kane. She let those sentiments show through in her voice as it projected throughout her ship.

"With the gathered talent we have aboard the question should be 'what *can't* we do?' *The William's Hunt* is like no chrono-ship in Naviwerks' armada. No other ship anywhere. We haven't just given her a name. We have given her an identity. Pride. Heart." A proud but grim smile curled the Captain's lips. "Making use of these qualities and the knowledge and experience most of us bring from our service to Naviwerks, we will go back in time, steal back what the corporation seeks to use to expand their power and control over the people of the world, and give them back to the rightful owners. Through this, we will expose Naviwerks and the CEOs so that eventually the world will rise up against them and demand recompense. Our actions will make them answer for their crimes."*Even if we are destroyed in the trying,* Alex thought. *The people will know.* "This is why I named her *The William's Hunt*. We will hunt Naviwerks with our cunning and our pride, and with justice on our side."

Alex fell silent for a moment to let that sink in. It wasn't a planned strategy designed to inspire her crew with the pause. Alex was no showman. She just seemed to do such things instinctively.

"This will not be easy, and if you hold any doubt in your conviction to these goals then I welcome you to depart the ship. No one would hold you to blame." Captain Alex felt she had to make the offer. Geri snorted quietly from where he leaned against the lockers, and shook his head. She gave her Security Officer a bland look, but all he did was grin in return. Even with his distrust of the Horotech he knew that the crew was devoted to her, and their purpose. He felt that her offer was in vain, and only to appease her conscience. Alex could read all of that in his expression, and found it annoying. She turned away from him as she continued.

"Naviwerks is only biding their time, monitoring the air for the signal that indicates an activated chrono-engine that is unauthorized. They know we have stolen their ship, and are aware that the tracking devices and systems that once tethered *The William* to their armada have been disengaged or removed all together. Their tactics will be to lock on to the signature energy waves of an engaged chrono-engine, predict a course based on those readings then send their own ships after us. Each craft will have on board at least one Agent under orders to capture or destroy us before we can harm their reputation."

Here, Alex grew hesitant again. This was a personal point for her, one she refused to allow to affect her commitment or judgment as Captain. She knew she must maintain that outward appearance of cold detachment and seem unaffected by outside influence. Memories once pleasant now haunted her, plagued those attempts, but she grasped on to those feelings and used them to enflame her conviction and devotion to the cause she created. They may be going to the past, but they didn't have to live in it. She inwardly reminded herself of that fact.

"These agents will be Tier 2 at the very least." The Agents of Naviwerks were ranked in tiers from five to one, the latter being the highest on the information ladder. Naviwerks would not trust anyone less than Tier 2 with confirmation of defiance against them. Their claws were not sunk deeply enough into Agents under that rank. They didn't have near enough condemning information on them and their families to keep them under control. "Before I left the corporation I had discovered enough evidence to lead me to believe that a program exists that gave them greater control over their high ranking Agents. I was unable to procure this information to be studied, but I saw enough to come to my own conclusions." Alex felt a spasm of pain within her heart to think of it, but she could not deny what she had seen before she had left Naviwerks. Human experimentation and genetic tampering was not something she could stomach easily, and had been one of the details that had convinced her to leave the corporation for good.

"The information suggested that the Naviwerks medical department had designed a nanotechnology that would give the CEOs the ability to influence the thoughts and motivations of their Tier 1 and 2 Agents." Alex hadn't understood half of the information she had stumbled upon, but a long evening in discussion with Dr. Hennessey had included terminology like *gene therapy*, *brain stem stimulation, perverted Horotechnology,* and *automatons.* Alex had felt more than a little sick after that. "These Agents will give us no quarter so expect none and above all else, do not underestimate the lengths they will go to in order to bring us to the corporation's idea of justice."

There. The warnings and reasoning had been given. Alex felt somewhat proud of herself for getting through it. It had been the first time she had said all of that out loud to the entire crew as their Captain. Oh, certainly she had said it all at the time she had recruited them, but the vernacular had been changed to suit their personalities. Her words had been chosen carefully to appeal to each of them. It had been manipulative on her part, and she knew it. But as bad as that was what was worse was that she did not regret it. She believed in this, and had known that deep down each member of her crew would agree with her. She had just had to reach inside of them, bring out that moral indignation until it burned in the front of their hearts and minds as it did within her own. This was just one more action a captain took that was unsavory, but necessary. Now that it was done, however, it was time to take the next step.

"Our first quarry is something Naviwerks wanted me to retrieve with my next assignment." Alex's voice took on a quality that was colder than it had been; the task would have been her first as an Admiral in Naviwerks' fleet. The promotion had been something she had strived for since her recruitment into the corporation, but it would have come with a price she was not willing to pay. The memory of the knowledge she'd gained about Naviwerks seemed painfully fresh to her, and affected her speech, colored it with disdain.

"In the late fifteenth century Leonardo da Vinci was commissioned by Ludovico Sforza to create the Gran Cavallo. The horse was the symbol for the aristocratic house of Sforza, and the statue was to be the largest cast bronze piece ever to be made." A few flicks of Alex's fingers across her control console brought up an image of the replica of the horse on the video monitors throughout the ship. "It was never actually made, as the bronze set aside for the statue was needed to make cannonballs for use against the invading French. However, it is believed that a test statue made to one-sixth scale was created in 1490, and then confiscated in 1499 by the Vatican after the French had used the full sized clay model as target practice."

Alex wasn't certain why Naviwerks wanted the scale model. There were no records of a museum or government agency wanting it retrieved, and to her knowledge, confirmed by Nigel, Da Vinci had no living relatives. She could only assume that it was one more acquisition Naviwerks wanted to have in their collection for future use. She intended to ensure that they did not have it in their possession, and had arranged a sale with Castello Sforzesco since it had been that ancestor who had commissioned the piece in the first place.

"Naviwerks' plan was to seize the model from the Vatican's soldiers after they had taken it, but before they reached the Holy See, some place between Milan and Vatican City." The image of the Gran Cavallo on the monitors blurred then faded out only to be replaced by a map of Italy circa the late fifteenth century. "For all of its greed and corruption, Naviwerks does try to adhere to the non-interference agenda. Altering history too blatantly could have dire consequences, obviously, so 1499 was to be their target destination." For all Alex knew, Naviwerks, disguised as Vatican soldiers, had made their mark on history with this action. They had done so before. "I intend to aim for a much earlier mark, that of 1490 when da Vinci was rumored to have made the model."

It was risky, and could possibly alter history. A lengthy discussion with Nigel over a fine bottle of brandy had convinced Alex and the Historian that the action wouldn't affect the time stream too much since it wouldn't change any of the major events of the French invasion, or the creation of the replica in the twentieth century. The scale model was still considered just a rumor, since the Vatican would not acknowledge the artifact publicly. Their greedy secrecy worked in Alex's favor this time.

"We will retrieve the Gran Cavallo directly from da Vinci's studio, return it to the present day and complete a transaction that I have arranged." The Castello functioned as a museum now with most of its works by Michelangelo, but they were very interested in da Vinci's scale statue and had offered a more than fair price. Captain Alex had sweetened the deal with a small bribe to keep the curator from making a counter offer to Naviwerks.

Alex glanced at the clock set in the controls in the arms of her chair as she muted the comm, then looked to her Pilot. "ETA to full green for flight, Miss Flynn?"

"Eight and a half minutes, Cap," came Angel's confident reply.

Alex nodded once then released the mute to address her crew once more. "Pre-flight will be completed in eight minutes. Shove off to commence in ten." Geri still looked doubtful of that time frame. Captain Alex's fingers hovered over the communications disconnect button, an eager smirk on her lips. "Captain Alexandria de Sade out."

The tick of a well-manicured but short fingernail against the control panel silenced the comm of *The*

William's Hunt.

"They'll be watching for the activation of the engines." Geri had a doubtful tone in his voice, but also a respectful one as well. "They'd be running those sensors looking for us since they noticed the ship was gone."

Captain Alex got a wicked lift of her lips as she looked at the controls on the arm of her chair. Mr. Reynolds had a very good point. *The William* may not be in their fleet any longer, but Naviwerks had technology that could detect the activation of a wormhole. Ostensibly, it was so they could keep track of their fleet; a safety precaution in case they needed to retrieve a ship that missed its return window. Naviwerks' tracking systems would have registered the location of extraction, cross referenced it with the log of the ship that had gone through and to what time, then sent another ship to tow back the lost ship. It was a convenient side effect that they could effectively retrieve a ship from any would be thieves, or in this case, pirates. They maintained their monopoly thusly, though it was not their only method. But there was one mistake that Naviwerks had made that Captain Alex had taken advantage of, one that rendered their sensors inadequate. They hadn't hired Mr. Kane.

Her gaze seemed to linger on an addition to the control console. It connected to a larger, more detailed control panel of switches, tabs and buttons in the engine room. Captain Alex wondered briefly if Mr. Kane had taken notice of it and the others yet. She had no doubt he would recognize them since they were of his design. Her index finger brushed over the frame work.

"At ease, Mr. Reynolds." Alex's voice was calm as she reassured her Security Officer. "Those circumstances have been taken into consideration." She lifted her focus from the console to Geri. One slender brow arched as if she dared him to continue to discuss the topic. He and Angel had helped her with the modifications to *The William*, but both of them were ignorant of what the additions to the engines would do. Even Captain Alex only had an academic knowledge of what all of Mr. Kane's designs did, but she had enough faith in his abilities based on what she had seen in action to trust what had not been tested. She had managed to test one application, but felt that her success had been something of a fluke, even luck. She wasn't eager to press that. Mr. Kane understood the operations better than she did. Let him impress the rest of the crew.

Alex didn't blame Geri for his doubts. In fact, she felt better to see them. Mr. Kane would be kept honest and on his toes thanks to her Security Officer's scrutiny. They would get the best efforts from their Horotech under such a watchful eye. Alex approved, and would allow it to happen. To encourage that she gave Geri a curt nod that Angel wouldn't see as she opened a line to the engine room.

"Mr. Kane," Captain Alex said into the comm. It seemed to take longer than it should for Laurence to reply, but Alex waited.

Geri wasn't quite as patient as his Captain. "The little twerp probably can't find the right switch to throw."

"Aye, Captain?" Laurence's voice sounded more proud than what they had seen of him thus far, and Alex

gave Geri a pointed look.

"ETA for full charge." It was more a demand for information than a question from Alex.

*"Ah..."*Laurence's pride fell beneath his typical uncertainty. *"Priming is at an optimum. Fuel cells are at full and, oh!"*He broke off in surprise. It was a few moments before he returned to the comm. Alex could imagine he had discovered one of the additions that were straight out of his notebooks. *"Oh, you have incorporated a magnifier. That will expedite things nicely. ETA for full charge in five minutes, Captain."*

On the bridge Alex gave Geri a smug look as she chuckled softly at the astonishment in Mr. Kane's voice. At the helm, Angel grinned around her chewing gum. Geri just sighed with his lips pressed together into a bland line.

"Thank you, Mr. Kane." Alex looked back to her console as if she could see the Horotech. That smug expression of hers didn't show signs of going away any time soon as she altered the comm link to Command mode. It would allow her to give orders with just a press of a control tab. She hoped that Mr. Kane remembered to switch off the voice activation on his end or the bridge would be filled with every little utterance from him.

The next three and a half minutes seemed to draw themselves out. The crew each had their own pre-flight duties. Alex didn't feel the need to check on their progress. With the sole exception of Mr. Kane, she had flown with each of them at one point or another, and knew them to be capable of accomplishing their tasks unsupervised. In the library, Nigel would be busy securing the bookcases, shelves and drawers that held his precious reference material. Dr. Hennessey, for as much as he had mocked Geri's efforts in the hold, would make certain his own inventory and supplies were safely locked and protected even though he would have done the very same thing twice before.

On the bridge, Geri settled himself into a chair near the network lockers, but not until after he double checked the Captain's and Angel's safety harnesses. Passage through a wormhole could be bumpy and unpredictable. The Security Officer took his duties to the safety of the ship, its crew and its cargo very seriously.

At a minute twenty seven seconds Captain Alex nodded to the back of Angel's head. "Open the bay doors, Miss Flynn."

The Captain swallowed against a moment of excitement that made the cords of her neck stand out. Her eyes stared straight ahead through the front ports where the ceiling of the warehouse in which they berthed began to retract. Her fingers curled against the arm of her chair. So much could go wrong within the next few moments. Naviwerks could be waiting for them in the skies. The addition of Mr. Kane's designs to the engines could cause a disruption in the wormhole and strand them in the places between now and then. She only allowed herself to entertain such thoughts until the countdown met one minute before she forced them to the back of her mind where they belonged.

"Mr. Kane, bring the engines online, if you please." Alex glanced towards Geri who nodded in return. He reached to the side where a monitoring station collected dust for lack of use. Internal visual monitoring was brought online, and the three of them in the bridge could see Mr. Kane move to his own console, a mobile harness attached to his back and waist.

"Aye, Captain." Alex saw his mouth move on the monitor as his voice came over the comm. Then the ship gave a small, forward lurch on its moorings as the primary engine turned over. Lights all throughout the ship brightened as full power was achieved and a low level hum filled the ship. *"Systems online. We have green across the board."*

A pleased smile formed on Captain Alex's face as her gaze locked onto Geri's. He returned it with a small, one sided smile of his own and a quiet sigh as he settled back into his chair. Alex turned her attention back to Angel, who brought her own systems to full function. "Navigation and Flight controls online, Captain. Full green. Bay doors retracted. Launch panels locked in place. Moorings release on your command. Thirty seconds." The Pilot's voice displayed the excitement that her Captain had kept silent. While they did have that test run under their belts, this was the real moment for all of them.

Alex's finger depressed the comm button to address her crew once more before flight. "Secure locations for launch." She released the button as her eyes went to the countdown on her chair display.

25...24...23 Her heart beat against her chest. She had captained launches a thousand times before, but this one would be the one she would remember forever. This was *her* launch.

19...18 Once they cleared that bay window they would embark on a journey that had never been taken before, but it was more than that. Alex's instincts told her that this launch meant so much more than she could possibly realize at this moment.

12…11…10

"Mr. Kane, angle the primaries for ignition."

"Aye, Captain."

7…6…5

"Miss Flynn, release the moorings."

Angel twitched her fingers against a switch, and the moorings retracted from the sockets on the ship with a *thunk* against the hull.

3…2

Alex's jaw tightened then her lips curled around the words she had waited to say for months now. "Shove off."

III
Milan, 1490

On Captain Alex's command, Angel's fingers ticked out the sequence that would fire the burners at full. The roar was muffled through the hull, but still loud enough to give a start to even the most seasoned crew member. Laurence was the exception in that his experience with flight was limited to commuter ships and simulations. Inside the engine room the primary engine burst into chemical-combusted life. The turbine, though muted by its casing, whined loudly. Most people would find the noise unbearable, but to Laurence it might as well have been angels singing. He could tell by the pitch and vibration that the engine was operating perfectly, which was proven half a moment later when the energy plume released through the external thrust funnels shoved against the launch panels. From there physics took over, and *The William's Hunt* burst out of the warehouse at launch velocity.

The same scientific law made Laurence lurch to the back of the engine room. If not for the mobile safety harness he would have knocked against the metal beams in the wall. He grasped onto the lines that connected the harness to the ceiling with both hands and a grunt to regain his footing. "Engage the pre-tensioners *before* launch, Laurence!" With a self-deprecating sigh, Laurence hit the button on the chest piece of the harness then felt the ceiling strands retract to the desired tension for flight. Then, since his services would not be needed until the Captain called for activation of the chrono-engine, he began a systems check to monitor the primary engine during flight. He already knew that the chrono-engine was in the green for activation, and he spared the dormant piece of equipment a fond glance.

On the bridge Geri barely restrained laughter after he witnessed the Horotech's mishap. Captain Alex slid him a bland glance with tightened lips, but her attention was drawn back to her Pilot as Angel spoke up. "All systems functioning at optimum levels." Amazement colored her tone of voice. Alex knew that the ship was operating better than average which would impress her Pilot. "Waiting for course, Cap."

"Three minutes full burn, Northwest," was Alex's reply. She smirked as Angel began to plot the course into the Navigation controls knowing that she would catch her Pilot off guard as she continued. "Then West full burn for five."

Angel was surprised enough that she actually glanced back over her shoulder at Captain Alex. Twice. Alex just gave her a clever look in return. In open confusion, Angel turned back to the Nav System and entered both in sequence with only the barest shake of her head.

"Mr. Kane." Alex raised her voice over the comm. She knew the noise of the turbine would make it difficult for Laurence to hear her.

"Aye, Captain?" The Horotech sounded as confused as the Pilot looked.

"The primary control panel for the chrono-engine holds a small red button with an X on it." Alex turned her eyes to the monitor Geri sat at, and saw Laurence scurry to the controls she indicated. He was caught visibly off-guard as he noted the variations to what should have been a familiar arrangement of knobs and switches. *"Aye, Captain. I see it."*

"On my mark, you are to press that button without delay."Her voice neither rose nor changed cadence.

"Aye, Captain," said Laurence with a note of curiosity in his voice. *"Standing by."*His neat and slender brows lowered into a fascinated frown as he eyed the strange little button. His finger rubbed under his lower lip as he muttered to himself, but since Alex had left the comm open it was heard on the bridge. *"Now what precisely do you do, my little friend?"*

Geri and Angel were both silent, but the Security Officer was able to look at Captain Alex as if he waited for her to do something very interesting. She in turn ignored his scrutiny. Patience would give Geri the answers he all but begged for with his eyes. She chose instead to look out at the sky as her ship cut through it, and a sense of pride welled up within her. It might be a bit premature, but her confidence was returning with a vengeance.

"Thirty seconds to first destination, Captain." Angel felt the nervousness that wasn't displayed by anyone else. It came through in her voice.

"Ready, Mr. Kane."Alex gave him the warning.

*"Aye, Captain."*Laurence replied. *"On your mark."*

Alex watched the countdown to destination on her control panel much the way she had with the launch. This one could afford to be missed by a second or two, but she preferred perfection. When the digits displayed zero she nodded as she gave the command. "Mark."

When she looked back to the monitor Alex could see that Laurence's fingers had begun to shake as he had waited for the command. They twitched before he pressed them to the red button. Immediately afterward he let out with a yelp that was heard over the comm as the chrono-engine pulsed to life then fell to stillness again. His attention snapped to the engine arrangement where the precious machinery had given a thrum.

Laurence looked back to the control panel in astonishment, but it was followed by sudden recognition. *"...dear God..."* Realization gave way to admiration then irritation. All of his thoughts played across his face one after another until finally his lips pressed together. He looked at the mesh speaker of the comm, but held his tongue.

Captain Alex's face held a smug expression as Angel turned the ship for the next course without the need to be instructed to do so. Her glance slid to her Security Officer who did not appear impressed. Alex arched a brow at him, but Geri said nothing.

"Captain," Angel's anxious voice called out.

"Sensors indicate a spike in chrono-energy at initial destination." This time she did turn to give Captain Alex a worried look.

"As expected, Miss Flynn." Alex, on the other hand, sounded unconcerned. In fact, she seemed satisfied. "Proceed to next destination at full burn, if you please."

Angel hesitated only a moment before she turned back to her consoles with a snap of her gum. The Nav systems were working properly so adjustments by her were unnecessary. All she had to do was monitor the flight, but her nerves prompted her to glance more often than she normally would to the monitor that tracked sky activity around them.

"One minute to destination, Mr. Kane," Alex called to Laurence. "Have the coordinates been set?"

Laurence had locked in the dates as soon as he had begun the pre-launch so was able to reply to the Captain with certainty. *"Aye, Captain. Activation is a go on your mark."* This time he remembered to mute the comm before he muttered under his breath. Alex saw his lips move on the screen, and could tell he was put out.

"Stand by." As long as he did as instructed Alex was prepared to deal with any display of annoyance. For now she turned a pointed look to her Security Officer.

Geri caught the stern look given to him by Captain Alex and knew that this destination would be the actual activation. Understanding dawned on him, and he snorted in wry amusement as he settled himself more in his chair.

Even Angel adjusted her harness as she called out the final countdown. “Miss Flynn, how are the skies?” Captain Alex interrupted the countdown, and watched as Angel looked more obviously at the monitor.

“The skies are clear, Cap.” Her Pilot seemed a little mystified by that observation, but was definitely relieved.

“On my mark then, Mr. Kane.” Alex looked to the monitor where she could see the Horotech watch the countdown on his own display. His hands were in position on the control panel. “In three…two…mark!”

Upon the Captain’s order Laurence threw the switch that ignited the chrono-engine definitively this time. His attention then snapped to the smaller but more important engine as it blazed into activity.

The light in the engine room grew almost blinding as the emissions from the chrono-engine became increasingly brighter. Laurence fumbled the brass-framed eye shields into place over his spectacles. A hum was felt more than heard throughout the ship. The low tone began in the chest then spread outward until it vibrated across the skin. It was disturbing in the least, but just before it became panic inducing the energy that built pulsed outward like a shot, and seemed to drag them all with it.

Captain Alex’s eyes went to the ornate analog clock on the wall of the bridge at that moment; it was a habit she had developed. Every trip she had taken into the past she marked the time of entry into a wormhole. It wasn’t necessary since every traveler worth their salt knew the clock stopped upon entry, and would start ticking again upon their return, but it was a novelty for her. *Quarter past eleven and thirty two seconds.* She burned the time into her mind then turned her attention to the forward windows.

Not that there was much to be seen as a ship traveled through the wormhole. The view was mostly over-bright white light with flecks of even brighter lights that winked in a dizzying display. Some felt nauseated to watch the transfer, and a few rare individuals had actually gone mad and claimed to have seen things in the wormhole. What they described before they lost the capability of speech were strange and horrifying creatures. Captain Alex had read the psych reports. Even with her cool, pragmatic mind she had been disturbed by the descriptions. The mind benders, as she called the psychologists, suggested that the effects of chrono-manipulation on a mind already prone to paranoia brought about these hallucinations which sent the unfortunates over the edge into madness. Alex wasn't certain if she believed that conclusion, but what she did know was that after her many journeys into the past she had not once seen anything in a wormhole to cause fear of that level.

The transfer was over with startling abruptness. One moment they were in the wormhole. In the next they burst forth into open air above a pastoral panorama. Everyone in the bridge was surprised to discover it was full dark instead of the late morning daylight they had left. Geri shot a look to the Captain, whose brows had lowered into slightly disapproving lines. It seemed their new Horotech was being creative, clever or absentminded. Captain Alex would find out which in due course, but there were other priorities to be seen to first.

"Mix the senses, Miss Flynn." Captain Alex's voice was tight as she gave the order. The chrono-engine would remain active in a low setting for the five day window. An adjustment of the energy output would put out a pulse that encouraged the mind to not pay attention to its location. A *you do not see me* suggestion to the nearby minds of animal and human alike. It was a design that Naviwerks engineers had created to avoid as much paradox as possible while in the past. A small pin attached to the collar emitted a small neural signal that synced the wearer's mind with the output. This would allow the crew to find the ship again once they had disembarked.

Angel adjusted the settings as instructed while Captain Alex looked out the windows with interest. "There." She pointed even though Angel wouldn't be able to see the gesture. "Three degrees to port."

"I see it, Cap." There was a copse of trees that would be suitable for concealment of *The William's Hunt*. It might gain a reputation for being haunted after their stay, but if they managed this as quickly as possible their presence might not leave a mark at all. Angel took over flight control to direct then land the ship by hand. The cover of darkness allowed her to take her time.

Angel lived up to her reputation. She gave them a smooth jaunt to the location and a steady landing. There was only a slight jar of the ship when the landing pads touched down. The primary engine was killed as soon as they were on the ground, which left only the slight hum of the chrono-engine.

Alex released the connections for her harness as she addressed the crew over the comms. “All hands to the Hold.” She stood from her chair after she disengaged the comms, but left her control panel activated. Angel and Geri released themselves from their harnesses as she affixed her rapier back on its lanyard on her hip. “Say nothing to Mr. Kane. Either of you.” She gave them both a firm look before she walked towards the stairs that led out of the bridge.

“No problem, Cap,” Angel replied with a flippant tone. “Wouldn’t know what to say anyway.” She was still confused about the mini-activation of the chrono-engine.

“Might be a bit hard to keep my mouth shut if the little twerp opens his. I didn’t like the look on his face, Captain.” Geri’s voice held an edge of warning to it. “Mr. Kane had looked ready to spit nails.”

“That is *my* concern, Mr. Reynolds.” Alex’s voice echoed back from the stairs down to the passageway. “I will handle it.” She knew there would be demands for explanations from both her and Mr. Kane. She intended to establish her authority now.

Geri sighed but didn’t argue. Alex had never thought he would. Her Security Officer would speak his mind if he felt she needed to hear it, but his loyalty to her was unquestionable. He had made that plain to many a hard head in the past.

They met Nigel and Dr. Hennessey in the passageway from their quarters to the Hold. The Historian gave a charming smile to the Ship’s Doctor. “Pleasant journey, wouldn’t you say old man?” He fell in step with the older doctor after he gave a nod to his Captain,

Angel and Geri. He placed a companionable hand on the man's shoulder, which was shrugged off instantly as the Doctor grumbled behind a handkerchief that was a lurid color of violet. Nigel tsked as he took his hand back. "Oh dear. Vomited again?" His tone was a mockery of sympathy.

Dr. Hennessey turned a dark look up at the taller fop of a man. "Get stuffed, Wellington." He ignored the chuckle that came from the Historian as he stumped down the passageway.

Dr. Hennessey at least held the lift for the rest of them. Once aboard, Nigel looked over the expressions of the bridge crew. "Safe to assume, Captain, that there is an interesting conversation in our near future with our good Mr. Kane?"

Captain Alex gave him a fierce look. "Now is not the time to bait me, Nigel."

After they reached the hold, Angel pulled herself up to sit on some boxes while Geri took up a position where he could see the lift, planted his feet, and crossed his arms.. Nigel took note of their positions before turning his smile to the Captain. "We are off to a wonderful start."

Alex gave him a withering gaze. She would prefer that this go smoothly and without incident. The less time wasted the less chance there was of something going wrong with their mission. Still, she was agitated with the desire to get going, and turned her impatient look to the lift as it rose away from the hold. She kept herself from pacing or any other display of her annoyance.

The lift lowered once more to reveal Laurence.

He barely waited for the machinery to come to a stop before he hauled open the lattice gate then stepped off the platform with more grace than he had shown thus far. Apparently, heightened emotions were good for his poise.

"Captain de Sade," Laurence said with conviction as he approached the group. His hazel eyes were locked onto the diminutive lady in authority. "I could not help but notice the alterations and additions to the engines, and I find myself wondering exactly how you procured those designs." He pointed at himself as he continued in quiet but clipped tones. "I know for a fact that they were never patented nor marketed since they are mine."

Angel's brows had lifted for the Horotech's temerity, and she glanced at Geri. His temper was legendary when it came to the Captain's defense. She was not going to move from her seat, but chewed her gum at a more rapid pace for how nervous this confrontation made her.

Geri cleared his throat as if to remind everyone of his presence. The warning went unheeded as Laurence stood before Captain de Sade with his arms crossed and an expectant look on his face.

Captain Alex looked up at Mr. Kane, but that was the extent of her movement. She didn't even deign to lift a brow at her Horotech. The truth was she felt his questions were within reason. They were his designs after all, and she hadn't paid a dime for them. That was not something she would admit to Mr. Kane, however. There was a precedent that needed to be set, and with her entire crew as witnesses she could little afford not to take advantage of the situation.

"Mr. Kane," she began with a calm but unapologetic tone. "Why do you think I hired you in the first place?" She smiled but it was chilly at best. It was the kind of expression a teacher might give a normally intelligent pupil who was being obtuse at the moment.

Laurence blinked with a deeper frown on his face. "Well, I would presume because of my talents, my accomplishment-oh!" He broke off as his mind caught up.

Alex saw dawning understanding come to Mr. Kane's face, and lifted her brows at him. Naviwerks had sent her to scout new Horotechs a few years ago. She hadn't forgotten the young awkward student that had caught her attention. But what his professors had told her about him was what she had recalled the most. He'd had wild ideas, fantastical notions and preposterous designs that would never function properly for very long even when his scholastic record showed that his designs were solid. The tests that he had been allowed not only functioned as Mr. Kane had predicted, but some even improved the performance of the chrono-engines. Unfortunately, Mr. Kane's personality tests and psych evaluations had all failed to meet Naviwerks' standards, and they had courted others, regardless of Alex's recommendations. But she had definitely not forgotten the young Horotech, nor his "wild ideas".

Laurence capitulated as he rubbed at the back of his neck. "Ah...yes, well. I see." He was mollified but still mildly put out. "I would still like to know how you managed to obtain the schematics."

"That is none of your concern, Mr. Kane."

Alex's answer was as firm as it was quick to be given.

Laurence's frown returned. "And what if I had refused your offer? Nobody besides myself knows how to operate some of those designs. You might have put your entire crew at risk."

"But you didn't," Alex countered as if she felt this entire conversation were a pointless exchange.

Angel's eyes went from Mr. Kane to Captain Alex and back as they exchanged words, almost as if she watched a tennis match. Geri scowled but remained silent as the Captain requested. Dr. Hennessey sighed with impatience, and Nigel watched them all with open amusement.

"But I very well could have!" Laurence lifted a finger in a shaky point at the Captain. "Piracy was not exactly my career of choice. The very thought of it threw my entire moral compass into a spin to the point where I had considered not even meeting with you." He blinked as he grew sheepish once more. "Captain."

The addition of her rank into the conversation assured Alex that she had Mr. Kane's loyalty, or at least his dedication to the cause. He might be put out to discover that she could and would do as she pleased when it came to her goals, but he was with her for the long haul. It brought a satisfied smile on her face. "And one day I might ask you to sit down with me to speak on what changed your mind, but not today." She turned her attention from Mr. Kane to include the rest of the crew. "For now, we have a job to do."

Alex walked towards the wardrobes and gestured for Nigel to follow. She located the ones labeled

Fifteenth Century where garb appropriate to their current time and location could be found. “Mr. Kane. Please explain our location.” She didn’t look back as she opened the wardrobe then began to pull out articles of clothing. This was her point of irritation. They should have come out at the same time of day that they had left. The fact that they hadn’t had surprised her, and she little liked surprises that she was not a party to.

“Ah…yes, of course Captain. Milan. 1490,” he answered with pride. Laurence cleared the catch from his throat as he clasped his hands behind his back. “Specifically June twentieth. Four thirty in the morning.” That was when the Captain turned back to look at him with lifted brows. “Give or take ten minutes.”He paused once more before his voice came out again but cracked and quiet. “A Friday.”

“Bull crap!” Geri growled out. “No one can hit a specific day let alone alter the time of arrival.” He huffed as he lowered his arms. “Most like you screwed up, and we’re two days ago.”

“Begging your pardon, but I can.” Laurence was as firm as possible as he answered Mr. Reynolds’ assessment of his skills. “And I have.”He crossed his arms in a gesture that was more nervous than confident. “I felt it better if we arrived under the cover of darkness, but near dawn. Since it is the Summer Solstice most country dwelling residents will not be working their fields, but seeing to their superstitions. Fewer eyes on the skies.”

Alex’s eyes glittered with her approval as she strode back towards Mr. Kane. A matching grin formed on her face. “It worked then.”

"Yes, Captain." Laurence turned to look back to her, and grinned in return. "Of course it did. I designed it."

Angel grimaced at the chuckle from Captain Alex. "What worked?" The heel of her boot thumped against the side of the box she sat on as if to get their attention. The truth was that she rarely was still, even when asleep.

Alex gestured for Laurence to proceed with an answer before she turned to go back to the wardrobe. It was his design, and she would prefer him to impress the crew himself.

Laurence blinked a couple of times before he spoke, and his hands rubbed together in a nervous motion before him. "One of the reasons why nobody could hit a specific date before, in fact the most they could hope for is the correct season they wanted, was that the chrono-engines lacked a certain…fine tuning, as it were. Well, you could, but you would have to be elbow deep in the engine at the time of activa-" he broke off as Geri cleared his throat again. Laurence glanced at him, swallowed then continued. "Yes, well. To make a long story short. I designed a tuner for the destination apparatus that allows me to target a specific date and time."He glanced at Captain Alex then. "Of course I programmed our destination out of habit. Not that I knew the tuner was installed until after."

Silence held sway in the Hold for a few moments before Geri broke it. "Bollocks," he growled with another huff. He eyed the Horotech before he moved to join the Captain at the wardrobes.

Laurence seemed to deflate in disappointment

that the crew were not suitably impressed. Dr. Hennessey watched the Horotech as Laurence gave a quiet sigh. He turned narrowed eyes to Captain de Sade and muttered, "Clever, clever woman taking on this lad. Naviwerks will never see him coming."

Nigel gave a dismissive wave of his hand in Geri's direction. "We will find out soon enough, and I dare say that I am looking forward to you eating crow, Mr. Reynolds." He grinned in the face of the glare the Security Officer gave him, but his chuckle was cut off as he had to catch the bundle of clothing Captain Alex tossed at him.

"That's enough." Alex gave them a stern look as she folded a dress over her arm. "Stop wasting time and get changed. Both of you. I expect you ready to go in ten."

"Don't suppose someone cares to enlighten us as to why we had two destination points, and why the first one triggered the chrono-engine?" Angel's curiosity was not going to be denied any longer.

Alex's clever pride was unhidden in her expression. "Tell them, Mr. Kane, as I am certain that you have reasoned that out by now."

Laurence's smile returned as he faced the crew with as much confidence as he could muster. "It's rather simple, really. By minutely activating the chrono-engine we laid down a marker. Anyone scanning for temporal energy manipulation signatures would key in on that activation." It wasn't how he had wanted that particular piece of engineering to work. Laurence had intended for it to act like an anchor point that might extend the window of opportunity for return from the past except the energy output was too small to truly alter the process. He and his professors had seen that design as a failure, but Captain de Sade had found a more devious use for it.

"And by the time they reached that location we would be at our real destination and through the wormhole."Nigel smiled at the Horotech, in a little more awe of the fellow. "Well done, Mr. Kane."

"It'll only work once," growled Geri as he tossed the garb he had chosen for himself over a thick shoulder. "They'll recalibrate their sensors to scan for any and all unauthorized activation in that area next time. Pick up on the real activation then all's they have to do is camp there for five days. Nab us when we come out."

"Once was all we needed this time, Mr. Reynolds," came Captain Alex's confident reply. She turned her ice blue eyes to her Security Officer with that clever smile still in place on her expression. "Next time we act just as cleverly, and even a Tier 2 Agent would have a hard time keeping up with us."She smiled at Geri as he grimaced in doubt, then she turned to go change her clothing. "Gear up, Mr. Reynolds."

"Captain..." Laurence's hesitant voice got Alex's attention. His smile was just as uncertain as he approached her. "Might I come with you?" His eyes and open face were hopeful even in the face of Mr. Reynolds' indignant huff. "I think I might be of some benefit to this venture."

"Oh?" Alex eyed the Horotech with curiosity. Not normally one to allow her body language to be so open, she thought to encourage Mr. Kane to speak his case. She arched a brow, and tilted her head as she shifting her weight over one hip. Nigel looked as though he might swallow his tongue as he attempted to suppress his amusement.

"Well," said Laurence a bit meekly as he rocked on his feet with his hands clasped behind his back. A slight blush colored his cheeks. "I speak Italian to begin with."

"So does Mr. Wellington," countered Captain Alex. She looked at Mr. Kane as he glanced towards Nigel. She was pleased to see him look back to her, and she gave him an impatient look.

"I'm sure, but does he speak fifteenth century Italian?" Laurence gave Nigel an apologetic look, but the Historian was more amused and interested than insulted. Since Nigel neither confirmed nor denied his fluency in old Italian, Laurence continued to explain himself to Captain de Sade. "You see,da Vinci was a requirement for the study of Horotechnology as some of his sketches indicate that he had come quite close to designing some fascinating devices far before their time." He grinned as he adjusted the spectacles that were perched on his nose. "It is really all quite fascinating, actually, especially since the master wrote in perfect mirror image. I wrote a paper on the possible ramifications of our current society should he have been ah-," He broke off with a clearing of his throat when he saw Captain de Sade lift a brow with an impatient drum of her fingers against the clothing over her arm.

"Right." Laurence sniffed once then smiled. "The point being that in order to properly understand da Vinci's designs one had to learn to read the language he wrote in, complete with vernacular and phrasing…and backwards. We students made a point of speaking to each other solely in da Vinci's Italian if only to confound our professors."

Captain Alex eyed Mr. Kane as she took this in, and mulled it over. It was obvious that the man had barely traveled from one city to another let alone spent any amount of time in the past. He was inexperienced, and unprepared for what waited for them a few miles down a country road beyond the ship. What stuck in her mind was that all of them had been in that very position once, and the only way to remedy that was with exposure. This was an important mission, being their first run, and there rested her hesitancy. She turned her head without taking her eyes off of Mr. Kane. "Nigel?"

The Historian closed his eyes as he shrugged a shoulder. "He has a point, my dear Captain. My Italian is strictly modern day. While I have read manuscripts and histories, I have never had occasion to attempt to speak it. It isn't as if Naviwerks allowed me to interact with the natives, if you will." An egotist he may be, but Nigel did not hesitate to admit a lack in his talents, especially to Captain de Sade. His honesty was one of the things that endeared him to her.

Alex nodded once before she faced Mr. Kane straight on again. "Very well. Find some garb that fits." She pointed off to end of the hold opposite the lift. "Changing chambers are there. Be ready and back here in ten."

Her will on the matter spoken, Alex turned for the chambers she had indicated, and started walking toward them. Enough time had been lost in dickering.

"Dr. Hennessey? You and Miss Flynn have the ship. I expect to find her in the same condition as I left her."

"The ship or Miss Flynn?" was Nigel's cheeky musing as he made to assist Mr. Kane.

The Doctor cleared his throat in what sounded like a resigned harrumph as he started for the lift. "Come along, girl. I'd like some tea while these four go traipsing the countryside." The purple handkerchief made another appearance to be brushed needlessly behind the man's neck.

Angel grinned around her chewing gum as she slid off the boxes she had perched herself upon. Her work boots thumped to the floor, after which she bounced into motion to follow the Doctor. "Good luck. We'll keep the heat on." She wiggled her fingers at the boys on her way past. The gesture earned her a roll of the eyes from Geri. Nigel blew her a kiss while Laurence just looked a little confused as he glanced over his shoulders from the wardrobe.

Alex smiled to herself as she watched the exchange. Yes, she had picked a good crew. Content with that thought she ducked into the wardrobe to change.

Captain Alex emerged not long after. The garb she had chosen for herself had been tailored to her after she had been promoted to the rank of Captain in Naviwerks' fleet. Her slight frame and less than average height had made it necessary for her to have her own wardrobe which she had made off with along with the chrono-ship and other supplies. She wore a forest green chemise beneath a deep brown v-neck bodice that stopped just above her waistline to be met by an over skirt of the same color that was slit from floor to knees. Tied to the bodice were slashed sleeves that allowed the chemise to show through as well. The garb was modest when compared with her captain's uniform, which showed off the form of her legs far more, yet it still brought out a feminism that was emphasized by her dark auburn hair that was left loose to curl and twist naturally.

Nigel and Geri were dressed and ready. They both had experience in donning the costumes. Alex knew that Geri had done many assignments in the past during his time with Naviwerks. Nigel hadn't, but she knew his taste for clothing extended far beyond his modern time. Both men looked at her, but only her Historian let his admiration show. She held a finger up at him as she passed by. "Not a word, Nigel."

Nigel held his hands up in surrender as he chuckled to his Captain. "Never again, madam. I recall quite vividly what happens when a man such as myself pays you a compliment. I still bear the scar, I believe."

Alex sighed. She knew that if she said anything more on the matter to Nigel it would only serve to bait him. He meant well, and she knew that his cheek hid a lot of the true man. She understood, kept his secret, and tolerated the rest. "Is Mr. Kane ready?"

"Ah..." Laurence's voice was muffled behind the door of the dressing chamber he occupied. "No. I seem to be having some difficulty with the doublet. The sleeves in particular."

Geri rolled his eyes before he moved to towards a chest of drawers. Nigel winked at Captain Alex then stepped up to Laurence's door. "They have to be tied on, Mr. Kane." He grinned as a shuffling noise could be heard throughout the hold from inside the chamber.

"And how, precisely, does one manage that?" asked Laurence with a note of desperation in his voice.

Amusement played across Nigel's face. "Did you tie them *before* you put the doublet on?"

There was a moment of silence before Laurence answered. "Oh good Lord."

Nigel laughed as he walked away from the chamber to rejoin Captain Alex. "That should speed things up, I think."

Alex couldn't keep a spark of entertainment from her eyes even if she did school her expression to a cold neutral. "At least you didn't offer to help him. I appreciate your restraint."

"Damn miracle," commented Geri as he unlocked one of the drawers. He used a key that hung from a ring that he kept on a chain around his neck.

"Nonsense." Nigel sniffed in mock indignation. "Self-control is just a thinly veiled martyr complex. Denial is such an ugly practice."

Laurence emerged from the dressing chamber. Alex hadn't thought it was possible for the man to seem more awkward, but he was now. The doublet was shorter than he would have liked since he kept tugging on the bottom as if that might help it fall farther than his upper thighs. A belt did nothing to help. The leggings he wore tied to the doublet, which would at least keep a stiff wind from destroying his modesty entirely.

He took one look at Nigel and Geri then let out a sound of dismay. "Oh I say! How is it that their garb is better fitted and more," he broke off with a cough as he blushed and tugged at the hem of his doublet again, "...covering?"

Geri wore a deep blue doublet that hung almost to his knees, and was held in place by a black tabard. It was militant in appearance which suited the Security Officer. Meanwhile, Nigel seemed to be able to wear anything, and make it look like the height of fashion. The Historian's green and silver patterned robe had more flowing arms with what looked like real fox fur on the cuffs and hem. Laurence joined them with as much dignity as he could manage.

Geri grinned at him."Nice knees."

Laurence gave the large man as much of a disinterested look at possible. It looked more as if he were dealing with a bout of indigestion.

Nigel couldn't contain his own sound of amusement. "Ignore him, Mr. Kane." Nigel shot Geri a wry look. "Or I will be forced to tout out photographic proof of Mr. Reynolds in the 13th century Scotland." Geri gave Nigel a look of warning, but the Security Officer was still too amused by the Horotech's appearance for it to be very effective.

"Enough." Captain Alex drew their attention to her, then arched a brow as Mr. Kane flat out stared in a manner that suggested he might never have seen a pretty woman before in his life. Fortunately for him, she appeared more amused than annoyed. When he realized what he had been doing, he cleared his throat, and looked away as his cheeks and neck took on a reddish color to match his doublet. Nigel's grin was given to Mr. Kane who seemed to be studying the toes of his boots, the floor, anything except Captain Alex who rolled her eyes at her Historian.

"Wellington." Geri's grumbling voice came out

a moment before he tossed a fabric bag to the Historian. The bag's drawstring was pulled tight, and it made a clinking noise as Nigel caught it.

The Historian pulled open the bag to examine the contents then nodded in satisfaction. "That will be plenty, I should think." He tied the bag to the inside of his robe. "Silver testones stamped between 1482 and 1486. Approximately twenty of them, Captain."

Alex nodded then turned for the panel that would release the gangplank. Her fingers plucked up the skirt of her dress in an expert manner that proved she was just as comfortable in a gown as she was in khakis, jackboots, and a military jacket. "Mr. Reynolds, give Mr. Kane a dagger and a pistol, if you please." She could feel the Security Officer's stare on her back as she entered the code to lower the ramp, but ignored it. All of them would need to be armed…just in case.

Geri frowned, but moved towards the weapons chest. He already had two swords in sheaths tucked under his arm, one of which was obviously Captain de Sade's rapier. It was a bit off date, but one would have to look closely to the hilt guard to know for certain. His own plasma pistol was hidden somewhere inside his doublet, but he pulled out another from the chest. It had a clever looking holster that was hidden behind the sheath of a chronologically correct dagger.

The Security Officer brought it up to Mr. Kane and shoved the lot against the Horotech's chest. Geri's eyes locked with Laurence's. "Replace that belt with this one, and only draw down if you absolutely have to. I will shoot you myself if I so much as think you didn't have enough reason to breach historical accuracy."

All the Horotech could do was nod in silent agreement then fumble with the belts to switch them out. After a final glare, Geri left Laurence to figure it all out for himself as he took the rapier to Captain Alex.

Once Laurence had the belt issue settled and stood next to Nigel, Captain Alex looked them over. Satisfied by what she saw, she turned to descend the ramp. “Keep together. Once we encounter locals Mr. Reynolds will act as the guard for our traveling group. Mr. Wellington is with me, and Mr. Kane is his brother. Do not embellish on this. Maintaining simplicity will make the story more believable.”

The first thing the group noticed upon stepped off the ramp into fifteenth century Italy was the smell. The nearby farms hosted animals of all sorts along with the humans who did not have the luxury of plumbing. Crops were fertilized the old-fashioned way and all combined, it made for an odor that could not be ignored whenever the early summer wind blew in their direction.

Alex had assumed that Laurence would be the one to comment on it, but it was Nigel who groaned and put a handkerchief to his mouth and nose. “Still not as bad as Tudor era London, but nonetheless...” He ignored the amused look Geri gave him.

Captain Alex led them to the dirt road she had spotted from the air, and by the time they arrived at the closest farm, the horizon had begun to lighten with the onset of dawn. Nigel and Laurence had worked out a fantastical yarn to present to the owner of the farm about their horse going lame back a few miles. Nigel would have preferred to have conducted the negotiations for a new horse and cart since he carried the money, but after a few quiet conversations, it was decided that Nigel's Italian truly was not up to fifteenth century snuff. So Laurence would be the one to approach the farmer. Nigel was able to at least instruct Laurence on what would be a fair price before handing over the bag.

Captain Alex, Nigel and Geri waited by the road while Laurence hailed the farmer who greeted him pleasantly enough in return. The Horotech and his predictable state of nerves began to tell the tale as agreed upon. The three on the road collectively held their breath as they watched on, but it all seemed to help the ruse. The farmer took one look at Alex, and agreed readily enough to the price Laurence offered. It was either sympathy for a woman on the road, or they overestimated what would be a good price for a horse and cart. Regardless, the farmer called for his younger son to bring a solid, if aging mare to be hitched and readied.

Laurence paid the man then returned to his companions, a triumphant smile on his face. "Well. That wasn't so bad." He handed the bag with the remaining testones back to Nigel who placed it inside his robe.

"Let us hope that the rest of this goes just as smoothly." Nigel gave Mr. Kane a smile in return while Geri and Captain Alex remained silent. The Security Officer wasn't one to celebrate prematurely, and Alex never trusted anything that went too easily.

The farmer's son led the horse and cart to them, but before he could dart back to his father Laurence held up a finger. With a calm smile on his face he asked the boy a question. It earned him a queer look in return, but the boy answered then ran off back to his father waiting in the field.

Nigel burst into laughter, and clapped Geri on the back of his shoulder. Even Captain Alex was smiling as Laurence helped her into the cart. Geri frowned at the Historian before he turned it on Laurence. "What."

Captain Alex was the one to answer Mr. Reynolds as she settled herself on the bench. "Mr. Kane asked the boy what the date was."

The Security Officer climbed up to take a seat next to her, then grabbed the reins up. His glare deepened on Mr. Kane who settled himself in the back of the cart. "And?"

Nigel's amusement had calmed to chuckles. "June twentieth." He grinned at Geri as he sat down across from Mr. Kane. "How would you like your crow cooked, my good fellow?"

IV
Hello, Alex

Agent Nash was crouched amongst some scrub on the side of a hill that overlooked the walls of Milan. It was mid-morning when they arrived. He had watched them come down the road in the cart then had shifted his position to one knee. With well-practiced movements, he removed from the sack beside him pieces of a rifle to assemble. All the while he kept his eyes on the target. Line of sight was perfect, but from this distance his point of interest was unclear. With steady motions the rifle clicked together piece by piece as the cart drew closer to his position.

The final piece to fit into place was the tubular sighting apparatus. He polished the magnifying glass on the end with a soft piece of chamois, and then put the rifle butt to his shoulder so he could peer through the sight. Some might find the motion of the world through the lens nauseating, but it didn't affect Nash as he swung the rifle from side to side until the passengers of the cart came into view.

He observed them for a few moments. Anger welled up within him to see them, the traitors. Other similar emotions tried to join that sentiment, but the neural therapy worked within his brain and suppressed them, as it was designed to do. Nash hadn't even noticed the adjustments. He simply made use of the focus that remained to load a plasma cartridge into the rifle. He would need only one.

He returned the rifle to his shoulder as he shifted his crouch to allow for recoil, and then he brought his target into view through the lens. He took a moment to admire her. Even Naviwerks and their nanotechnology couldn't eliminate basic human behavior, and she was certainly worth a second look. But that didn't change the fact that she was a renegade, a thief, and would-be pirate. His orders were clear.

His finger slid through the trigger guard and curled around the small metal arm as he took aim. "Hello, Alex."

BLAM!

Brought Up Short

V
Captain Alex Has Been Shot!

"Alex!" Geri Reynolds threw protocol to the winds when his Captain slammed into his side. The horse shied, but Geri ignored it, drawing his pistol as he shielded her body from further attacks with his massive torso. The bench on the front of the cart was far too vulnerable to another shot.

His sharp eyes tracked the probable trajectory of the shot, and he swore when he saw someone scrambling over the ridge of a nearby hill. From this distance he could not make out any details other than a flash of yellow and blue striped clothing.

"Geri," came Nigel Wellington's concerned voice from behind the bench. He had come to the front of the cart in an effort to assist Captain Alex, but could not get to her through Geri. The problem was, Geri did not seem to hear him or was not paying attention.

"Mr. Reynolds!" Nigel raised his voice, and his hand came to rest on Geri's shoulder which snapped the Security Officer's attention to the ship's Historian.

Nigel met Geri's eyes with his own pale brown eyes calmly, but firmly. "We need to assess the Captain's injuries, but to do that you have to stand down." Then his eyes went to the pistol in Geri's hand. "And put away the decidedly *not* fifteenth century weapon before you cause a paradox." He looked back into Geri's furious face, and smiled a little. "Please."

But it was not Nigel's insistent logic that got through to Geri. It was the petite, bloody hand that pressed weakly against his chest along with the wavering voice that came from beneath him. "Get off me, Mr. Reynolds, and stand down." Even in pain, Alex was thinking. There had not been a second shot. The sniper was not intent on following through on the attempt.

Geri hesitated just long enough to scan the hillside once more then reluctantly rose, and just as reluctantly slid his pistol back into the modified holster. "One shooter, Captain. East. Rising sun at his back. Too far away to pick out details, but I think I recognized the Papal Swiss Guard uniform."

Alex grimaced with her teeth clenched tightly together as Geri lifted off of her. Her right hand was pressed against her side, blood staining her skin and dress.

"Thank you, Mr. Reynolds." Her voice was clipped and quiet. "Get control of the horse, if you please."

Laurence Kane, the ship's newest crew member, clambered out of the back of the cart instead. "I'll do it." He gave Geri a worried look as he came around the side. "No offense, Mr. Reynolds, but you are liable to spook the horse more with the mood you are in." He swallowed hard for the sharp glare the Security Officer shot him, but was relieved to be out of the way for a different reason entirely. The sight of blood made him queasy.

"Switch places with me, old man." Nigel put his hand on Geri's shoulder as he started to climb into the front of the cart. "And let's see how marred our dear Captain's pretty skin is, hmm?" The Historian smiled in the face of Alex's snarl, but she gingerly sat up more on the bench. Nigel was not a medic, but Naviwerks, his former employer now nemesis, had given all of their employees training in basic first aid which, up until recently, included the whole crew of *The William's Hunt* except for Laurence Kane. As soon as Geri had maneuvered himself into the back of the cart Nigel settled himself into a stiff perch on the bench next to Captain Alex. The artful mess of his light brown hair was usually a source of pride to him, but right now it was annoying. He raked it out of his face with his fingers for an unobstructed view.

To look at her, Alex appeared to be more irritated than in pain, but Geri knew the signs of a deeper injury. The tension in the corners of her eyes, and the way the muscles of her jaw worked spasmodically as she clenched and unclenched her teeth in time with her heartbeat. Geri and Nigel shared a look, and Geri relaxed as Nigel took note of all of these signs, and dubiously dubbed them good.

Geri watched as Nigel peered through the hole in Captain Alex's dress. The blackened edges proved beyond a doubt that this was a plasma round. Someone from their own time was here, and gunning for their Captain. It was inevitable that Naviwerks would catch up with them, but not on their first run. No one could have known that they were coming to this exact date. The math involved in such guess work as that could make a statician's mind hurt.

"Plasma shots can be messy on the inside, but the pool of blood forming behind her tells me that the shot went through cleanly." Nigel said. He nodded to the back of the cart. Indeed, there was a matching hole through the side boards where Laurence had been sitting. They were lucky they did not have two injured crew members.

"And?" Geri pressed him for more information.

"And." Nigel gave Captain Alex a gentle smile as he loosely wrapped his hand around the side of her arm. "I would say our good Captain was a very lucky woman." His smile became a smirk as she growled quietly at him. Something about what he could do with his luck that sounded physically impossible.

Nigel continued. "The shot passed through cleanly, and I am certain I can stem the bleeding, but we will need to get her back to Dr. Hennessey as quickly as possible." He looked to Geri in the back of the cart. "I'd like to move her to the back where she can lay down for the return to the ship." As he and Geri prepared to move the Captain, Nigel gave her a look of warning. "This will not be comfortable, my dear, but I have faith in your stubbornness."

"Just get on with it, Nigel." Alex's voice was tight and clipped. She despised showing weakness of any sort. She would be in a foul mood for weeks for this, and the grip she had on Geri and Nigel gave warning to that. Fortunately, they both were familiar with her moods and paid it no mind.

As they settled the Captain as gently as possible in the back of the cart, Laurence kept hold of the horse's bridle. The nag's head was pulled low and against his wiry chest in an effort to keep the beast calm. He watched the action in the cart, his brows creased upward, and he began chewing the corner of his lip. This was certainly turning into quite the trial by fire. It was possibly a good indication of what they could look forward to in their new endeavors. And yet, he didn't find himself regretful. Frightened and concerned for the Captain, surely. But rethinking his decision to be here? Not one whit, which seemed odd to him.

From where he was calming the horse at the front of the cart Laurence nervously spoke up. "Ah… pardon, but…the road is bound to have more travelers on it than before since the day has progressed. They are certain to notice something amiss. Perhaps offer assistance. What shall we do?"

"The same thing we always do under these circumstances." Geri settled himself on the bench, and jerked his head to the empty seat next to him as he took up the reins. "Plague."

Laurence blinked with his mouth agape as he stared at the Security Officer. Then the startled Horotech scrambled for the bench before Geri had to make a second request. "Plague. Really?"

Behind them Nigel chuckled quietly. He had the Captain's upper body pillowed under his leg. His over tunic had been removed for a compress over the entry and exit wounds on Captain Alex's side. "Standard Naviwerks protocol for emergency situations when traveling within a century or two after an outbreak of the plague. It guarantees that any well-intended bystanders lose any and all interest in being a Good Samaritan."

"Oh. Yes, well I can see how that would be an effective deterrent." Laurence gripped the seat of the bench as Mr. Reynolds turned the cart around. A muffled grunt from the injured Captain protested the rough handling, but Geri didn't slow.

Geri intended for them to make better time back to the ship than their arrival. It would make for an unpleasant trip for Alex, but he knew his Captain. She would prefer that they be safe than comfortable "You watch. After one or two people the road will be cleared between here and the ship." He hated doing it, but he snipped the horse on the backside with the reins and got them moving at a good clip.

It only took a few minutes for circumstances to prove the Security Officer right. Soon enough some passerby caught sight of Alex in the back of the cart with Nigel obviously giving aid. When they made to approach to offer help Laurence got a nudge of Geri's elbow, and he warned them to come no closer, telling them their passenger was displaying signs of the plague. Their would-be saviors crossed themselves, covered their nose and mouth with a piece of fabric, and made a sign to ward off evil as they quickly backed away. As predicted, word spread down the road, and the cart found a clear, swift path.

Once Captain Alex was as comfortable as he

could make her, Nigel glanced over his shoulder towards Geri on the front bench. "As soon as we have the Captain back to the ship we need to tell the contract holder of the delay in fulfilling our end of the bargain." His tone said that he intended on doing that himself since Captain de Sade would be laid up.

"Bugger that." Geri spat to the side, but didn't take his eyes off the road ahead of them. "Let him hire Naviwerks if he wants the damn statue so bad." Nigel couldn't see it, but Laurence next to Geri in the front saw the stubborn set to the Security Officer's jaw.

"I doubt very much he would approach them after this," Nigel replied. "The Corporation obviously knows what we are about if they had a trap laid. We know what they are capable of. How many people have disappeared into some unknown point in time simply because they crossed Naviwerks? They certainly wouldn't hesitate to torture the contract holder for information at the very least."

"All the more reason we don't finish this," said Geri with a growl in his voice. "And we tell the mark to forget the model. They ain't seriously missed it all this time. They can do without it."

"Wait." Laurence looked back at Nigel, eyes wide. "What? Are you suggesting that Naviwerks…"

Nigel nodded to the Horotech. "Left people five days in their wake."

All three of them were familiar with the time limits inherent in the chrono-engines. The machine could only maintain the entrance of the wormhole for five days. If a Naviwerks chrono-ship got stranded in the past for lingering their flight records would indicate them as overdue, and the Corporation could send a tow ship to retrieve them. But it became a very effective threat to any malcontent or troublemaker to "be left five days in our wake".

"I seen it happen," said Geri with a tone of voice that was grim even for him. "Went out on a run once. Wasn't Captain Alex's. Ship's Historian was a hassle. Kept naggin' at the assigned Agent about paradox and protocol." His eyes stayed glued to the road. "Agent wasn't listening, and went out in non-period clothes. Raised a hullabaloo in the town enough we lost the target, but the Agent blamed the Historian. Instead of going back to original chrono-location which would give the man a chance to file a report the Agent tossed him from the hold and ordered the Captain to reverse engine."

"Th-that's.." Laurence sputtered.

"Morally unsound? An irresponsible use of power?" Nigel's expression hardened. He knew that Laurence had repeatedly failed to get a position on the Naviwerk's team of Horotechs, the engineers who specialized in chrono-engines. "My dear man. Why do you think we all divorced ourselves from the Corporation to sign on to piracy with Captain Alex?"

The Historian watched as Laurence looked from him to Geri. The Security Officer glanced at the smaller man, and gave him a curt nod before turning his eyes back to the road.

"Regardless, we must complete the contract so that word spreads that people have an alternative to Naviwerks for retrieving lost heirlooms. We will simply have to wait until our Captain is on her pretty little feet again."

"And I'm tellin' you no. We don't." Geri's voice wasn't raised but it was getting harsher. "We need more in the way of security measures before we go up against the Corporation again. Better plans. Especially since they know we're active. Any rep we make for ourselves ain't going to do a lick of good if we're dead."

"And *I* am saying that we could do these things while Captain de Sade heals." Nigel's voice gained an impatient tone, and his lips snapped together into a thin line.

They had just reached the copse of trees that hid *The William's Hunt* when the Captain spoke up. "… enough...!" Her voice was weak from blood loss and pain, but sharp enough to get both men's attention. "We do not abandon our contracts."

Angel Flynn must have seen them approach on the sensors, and had the Hold's gangplank open with Dr. Hennessey on alert by the time they reached the ship. The ship's Doctor was waiting just inside with his leather medical case tucked under his arm while the pilot brought a gurney from his wing.

Geri continued to argue as he halted the cart by the base of the gangplank. "With all due respect, Captain, I-.."

Captain Alex cut him off with a snarl. "We do *not*. Under any circumstances. Abandon a contract. Am I understood Mr. Reynolds?"

The Captain's forehead creased in pain, and she fell limp against Nigel, who gently brushed some stray dark auburn locks of hair from her forehead. "Easy,

Captain. Why don't we revisit the discussion after Dr. Hennessey has had a chance to practice his excuse for medicine on you, hmm?"

Laurence stepped quietly out of the cart to slip out of the way. He watched Dr. Hennessey humph his way down the gangplank to the cart. Even that short bit of exertions had the portly man out of breath. It wasn't that the Doctor was obese, but when compared to the slender Horotech, Dr. Hennessey was of decent girth.

The Doctor glared at Geri and Nigel as he passed them by. A firm wiggle of his finger beckoned Nigel forward. "Bring her to me carefully, Wellington."

What happened next seemed to Laurence a series of well-orchestrated but hurried maneuvers that centered on the crew's obvious concern for Captain de Sade. It amazed him how much they all rallied around the small woman. He knew they were loyal to her, obviously, or they would not have signed on to piracy with her, but watching them all it was quite plain that they cared for her, each and every one.

Oh, they all showed it differently. For instance, Geri hid behind his roughneck personality, but his eyes spoke of more concern than was evident at first glance. It could explain why it was said that he never spoke an ill word, or showed the Captain anything less than the highest respect possible.

Even Dr. Hennessey was taking Captain Alex to task for not ducking fast enough, and what has he told her about her choice of occupation turning her into a walking target? But, the corners of his lips held a fondness that would have easily been overlooked if one was not paying attention. Angel? Nigel? They were the same, and in spite of the circumstances, Laurence found he wanted to smile a little at his observations. Perhaps he hadn't made a mistake in accepting this position. Perhaps there were reasons for his earlier lack of regret.

"All right." Dr. Hennessey finished packing the wounds temporarily with cloth treated with a coagulant retardant after an initial inspection. "Let's just keep the wound bleeding to naturally wash out any foreign objects that might have gotten into it." As he backed away from the cart he flapped a hand in Captain Alex's direction, and jerked his chin down as he skewered Geri and Nigel with a look. "You two. Settle her on the gurney and get her to medical."

The Doctor took Angel by the arm, and pushed her gently in their direction. "Go with them, and do whatever you must to keep her awake. Don't want her falling asleep until I say so."

His eyes fell upon Laurence, much to the Horotech's surprise. "Come with me, boy. Might need an extra pair of hands, and I notice that you happen to have a couple." The Doctor pulled out his handkerchief which he used to wipe blood from his hands as he stumped back up the gangplank. He obviously expected Laurence to follow.

Laurence glanced back to the cart where Geri and Nigel were carefully transferring Captain Alex to the gurney, then hurried to catch up with Dr. Hennessey. The man was using the same handkerchief to mop at his brow that he had used on his hands. The Horotech couldn't help but check to be certain the Doctor hadn't smeared anything unpleasant across his face, but mysteriously there wasn't a trace.

Laurence kept his voice low even as they hurried through the hold to the lift. "Will she be all right, Doctor?"

Dr. Hennessey waved his hand at Laurence, his brow furrowed and his lips pressed together. "Yes, yes. She will be fine. Plasma rounds are nasty business, but Wellington had the right of it. Just need to close her up a bit. Tank her up on what blood she has lost." He gave a sharp huff as he closed the lattice gate to the lift with a rough gesture. Not half a heartbeat later he got them moving with an emphatic manipulation of the toggle.

Laurence paled for the mention of blood, and felt that the lift was moving faster than normal.

"She'll suffer through a few injections, which she won't like, but too bad. She hired me on, and what I say goes in the medical department." He punctuated that with a harrumph. "That was our agreement."

The Doctor's statement might have taken Laurence aback if not for the worry lines that creased the edges of the older man's eyes. He was certain that the man meant every word he said. But this incident had distressed him more than Laurence expected. Who was Captain Alex to these people on an individual basis to instill such a depth of caring in them? Laurence was beginning to think his level of ignorance about the woman was far greater than he assumed.

He put a hesitant hand on Dr. Hennessey's shoulder in a gesture that he hoped was reassuring. Laurence knew his social skills were less than polished to say the least, but he did try. "I am confident in your abilities to get our good Captain back on her feet.

Thank you."

Dr. Hennessey glanced at the hand on his shoulder. His thick, grey brows came down as his lips tightened together, and he turned on Laurence.

"Well, I am so relieved to know you have faith in my skills." Quick, sharp brushes of his fingers shooed the hand from his shoulder. "My self-esteem was feeling neglected." The lift came to a halt, and he reached out to yank the lattice gate open, stumping forward swiftly. "Now if you are finished offering empty and unnecessary platitudes, we have work to do. Step lively, Mr. Kane."

Laurence yanked his hand back. *So much for trying to be friendly*, he thought. It was immediately followed up by *Will I ever fit in with the crew?* He suppressed a sigh as he followed Dr. Hennessey.

The medical wing looked much the same as the rest of the ship, until he saw Dr. Hennessey's clinic. Organized chaos was the only way to describe it. The room was roughly the same size as the mess hall, but the amount of cabinets, trays and moveable tables made it seem smaller.

The cabinets were obviously old, and just as obviously were recent additions to the ship since their carved oak doors did not match the rest of the décor. A closer look at them revealed that they were finely crafted reproductions of Greek carvings and reliefs, including the entire Oath of Hippocrates in Greek with the man's portrait in the upper left corner. The countertops were a dark grey marble with black and amber veining. Brass fixtures decorated the cabinet and drawer handles as well as the spigots for the sinks.

Everywhere were various instruments, scopes, scales and other items Laurence could not immediately identify. There was an exam table in the center of it all made of what looked like the same material as the hull. Gears, hinges and hydraulic arms made it easy for Dr. Hennessey to adjust it for whatever he needed. Thick padding covered with stiff bleached leather made it look comfortable for the patient. Descending from the ceiling were more brass-coated hinged arms holding an overhead light panel. Connected to that were more instruments with various tubes attached to their ends that in turn disappeared into the ceiling. The floor was tiled to match the counter tops, and everything…absolutely *everything*…was spotless and shining clean.

Laurence realized that Dr. Hennessey considered this his haven as much as Laurence did the engine room. His understanding and respect for the man went up just a little more.

Dr. Hennessey immediately approached a set of drawers. He pointed off to the other side of the room without looking as he grumbled at Laurence. "Over there, boy. Middle upper cabinet. There is a tray wrapped in cellophane on the second shelf. Pull it down, and place it on one of the carts." The Doctor seemed to have a catalog in his head of where everything was since he was removing items from drawers without having to search for them.

Laurence went to the cabinet and found what the Doctor requested. He pulled down the tray then blanched a little when he saw what it contained: needles of various sizes, lengths and shapes; scalpels and knives; sutures of different material; probes; prods;

clamps; cloth, etc. His imagination conjured all manner of ways the instruments could be used that probably had nothing to do with actual medicine. He set the tray on one of the rolling carts as directed then backed away as if it might bite him. "Uh…there you are, Doctor." Laurence swallowed against a bout of nausea, and hoped that the good Doctor didn't ask for him to assist. "Is there…is there anything else?"

"Yes," said Dr. Hennessey as he turned around with a tray of his own that he had just put together. "Get out, and stay out of the way." He skewered the Horotech with a sharp glare, one bushy eyebrow lifted. The Horotech swallowed again then backed out of the clinic with a nod.

Just in time, since Geri and Nigel came around the corner pushing the gurney that held Captain Alex. Angel was keeping up with them, smiling down at her Captain with a lock of her mousy hair that had slipped the ponytail dangling in her face, and was obviously mid-story. "-…downright awful, you were. You kept pegging the tachometer until the Captain thought you'd blow the transmission, or at least a shaft." Angel's chuckle was softer than Laurence would have expected from the tomboy pilot.

The Captain didn't seem to share her amusement, however. "..would have been fine…if that old man had greased the gears…once in a while.."

"You clipped the wing against a wall, Alex." Angel grinned, but she had to step away. The door to the clinic was only wide enough to allow the gurney through with Geri and Nigel before and after.

The Pilot was left in the hallway with Laurence,

and to his surprise, she grabbed his arm with both hands. Her attention was held solidly by the bustling men inside the clinic, but Laurence could see that her deep brown eyes were a bit shiny. With a sympathetic smile, he shifted position so he could put an arm awkwardly around Angel's back. She went with it, but continued to grip his free hand. Hard. Laurence's smile became something of a wince.

Gently but swiftly, Geri and Nigel transferred Captain Alex to the exam table. A small sound escaped her for the jostling, but as soon as she was settled, Dr. Hennessey placed a hydro-spray into her neck. Laurence assumed it was a combination sedative and painkiller since a moment later the Captain relaxed, and the pain creases smoothed away from her expression. Dr. Hennessey replaced the hydro-gun with a pair of scissors which he waved absently at Geri and Nigel. "You two. Out. She wouldn't thank me for giving you a free view of things you ought not to see."

Geri might have turned a slight shade of red, but since he swiped a hand over his features it was difficult to tell. Nigel's brows lifted almost indignantly, but he didn't say a word. He just turned for the door, and pulled Geri with him by the front of his tunic.

Dr. Hennessey looked past them into the hall with a scowl to gesture at Laurence and Angel. "Miss Flynn! I want you in here to assist. You have the smallest fingers, and she won't care if you see her. Hurry now! She's waited long enough." He quickly turned back around to see to Captain Alex. "And close the door behind you."

Angel patted Laurence's arm as if he were the

one that needed reassuring. A small, tight smile crossed her face as she walked away to slip past Geri and Nigel. As soon as she was in the room the door was shut quietly, but firmly. That left the three men standing in the hallway staring at the clinic door.

They stood in silence for a few moments. Nigel was the first to come to his senses, and he placed a hand on Laurence's and Geri's arm. "Come on then, gentlemen. Let us leave our Captain in Dr. Hennessey's capable hands. We have things to discuss." He gave them a tense smile before starting back down the hall.

Laurence and Geri shared a perplexed look. It changed quickly into a disapproving scowl just before the ship's Security Officer marched after Nigel.

Laurence dearly hoped that Nigel would be willing to do most of the talking. Geri intimidated Laurence beyond belief. For one wild moment he thought about hiding in the engine room until the other men came to a decision, but he knew that if he ever wanted to be considered a full member of the crew, he had to step up. He sighed softly, and went to catch up with the men.

They descended back into the hold of the ship. None of them said a word until everyone was comfortable. Geri planted both feet with his arms crossed over his chest, and a dour expression on his face. Nigel looked worried, but determined where stood next to a metal support pillar. Laurence couldn't seem to decide if he wanted to lean, shift from foot to foot, arms crossed or not, and none of them seemed to want to be the first to speak. Finally, Nigel took the lead.

"We must resume our mission," Nigel began

with a sharp look at Geri, "per our Captain's orders." He pointed at Geri with a slender finger. "And I dare you, sir, to suggest that she was addle-minded from pain."

Geri frowned even more, but didn't dare follow through on the Historian's challenge. The entire matrix of the universe would have to change before he even hinted that Captain Alex had some sort of shortcoming. "You want to leave *him* to guard the ship?" As if the derogatory tone in his voice weren't enough to indicate who he was talking about, he jerked his head in Laurence's direction.

Nigel didn't change his expression, but he did roll his eyes. Having worked with Geri before, the Historian had gained a few skills on the matter. "I thought to bring him along to translate, actually. As in the original plan. Mr. Kane is the only one who can speak archaic Italian." He held up a hand to forestall Geri's protests. "Miss Flynn is quite capable with a plasma rifle. I have no doubt that she will adequately protect the ship and our Captain, Mr. Reynolds."

Geri's jaw worked as he ground his teeth together. Frustration, worry and anger were taking their toll on the Security Officer, and it was beginning to show. "That shot came from a plasma rifle. Not like what we have on board. Judging by the distance, it was high powered and accurate." His eyes locked on the Historian's. "State of the art. Only people I know that own those kinds of weapons and could be back here are Corporation. Naviwerks knows we're here. They could be waiting for us in the city."

Laurence's heart beat picked up its pace. *Good*

Lord, he thought. *I've been a pirate less than a day and already the time-travelling equivalent of the East India Trading Company is after me!* His hand went to his neck as if he could already feel a noose around it, but he continued to listen.

Nigel nodded, but his expression was still firm. "We all knew this would happen. It just came sooner than expected, and I for one thank God. I'd rather get it over with so we can move along and adapt." He eyed Geri with a challenging look. "That said, however, it was one man, not an entire patrol of Agents. I think it is safe to assume that they underestimate our determination."

Geri's brows came down thoughtfully. Laurence was glad to see it. It meant that the Security Officer was using his mind instead of reacting on pure adrenaline and anger.

"What do you mean?" Geri's voice was still gruff, but the edge of panic had left it, at least.

"Think about it, man" Nigel said with a slight gesture, one that a teacher might give to encourage a student to work a problem through for themselves. "One Agent. In the Papal Swiss Guard uniform, you say?" At Geri's nod Nigel continued with a small but growing smile. "They believe they have the upper hand, can intimidate us into retreating, and obviously will not be in Milan."

Laurence tilted his head as he chewed on the inside corner of his lip. The reasoning was sound if he was following Nigel well enough.

"I don't get it," said Geri. His nostrils flared as he took a deep breath, and the cords in his neck stood out a little more.

Nigel chuckled as he stepped closer to the Security Officer. Their height was near equal, as it turned out, and Nigel only had to look up a little to meet the other man's eyes. "My good man. They will assume that we will abandon our mission to see to Captain de Sade. Not to mention that The Papal Swiss Guard belongs in Rome. The Holy See, to be specific." Mischief glinted in his light brown eyes. "And were not officially created for another sixteen years."

Geri had initially given the Historian a look of warning for invading his personal space. The man was a Molly. Geri had nothing against such a lifestyle, as long as it stayed out of his. But Nigel's last statement made the Security Officer blink, then lower his arms.

"They made a mistake?" Geri asked in astonishment.

Nigel spread his hands with a slight shrug of his shoulders. "Oh, I doubt that, knowing the level of information their Historians have access to," his expression grew sly. "But I do find it interesting that they were willing to take such a risk with something so chronologically misplaced. It is possible that you yourself made a mistake in what you think you saw."

He stepped back. "Regardless, they will not be in Milan. I would bet my scrolls." Everyone who knew Nigel knew that he did not risk his precious reference collection lightly.

Geri paced away from the other two men in silence. His hand smoothed over his mouth as he thought this through. Naviwerks was steadfast in their operations. One did not alter history. One did not deviate from the time period one would be in. So why were they breaking their own rules? Geri was not mistaken in the flash of yellow and blue stripes he saw on the retreating man. Even though the rising sun had been facing him that detail had stood out.

"They control the Guard." Laurence's voice filled the silence. He said it with a hesitant tone, but there it was, and he swallowed nervously as both Nigel and Geri turned to look at him with expressions that clearly said he should explain himself.

"Well, it only makes sense," he offered with a slight tremor in his voice. "Why else risk exposing such a high profile entity as the Papal Swiss Guard before their official existence if they did not feel they could control the situation? At this time it was the church that chronicled the happenings. No one would gainsay what they wrote down as the truth." Laurence began to blink more rapidly, and his fingers fidgeted as the Historian and the Security Officer closed in on him, Nigel in fascination, while Geri looked like he was growing impatient again.

Laurence continued. "So to them it wasn't a risk. Look, I'm simply following a line of logic. You needn't look at me like that, Mr. Reynolds. If I am wrong then it still makes sense that more Agents will not be in Milan waiting for us since w-…"

Nigel raised a hand. "No, I believe you are correct." Oh, their little Horotech was cleverer than Captain Alex led them to believe. His mind was sharp indeed. He had his own growing reasoning for why it made sense for Naviwerks to have Agents in the Papal Swiss Guard if not outright control of the group. It would mean far darker dealings within the corporation than any of them had guessed, and Nigel wasn't willing to commit to the hypothesis just yet so he kept these thoughts to himself for now. "But perhaps this mystery is one we should pursue at another time. Right now we have a model to obtain. Then we can return to berth where we can puzzle this."

Geri frowned at Laurence, thinking things through while Nigel had his say. He had been convinced to finish their mission, but only because that had been their Captain's orders. All of this Papal Guard and Corporation guesswork was doing nothing more than muddy his thoughts. He would let the Historian and Horotech figure it out then form his own opinion once they had more solid facts.

"Fine." He turned to stomp off towards the wardrobes. "Wellington. Change clothes. Ours are bloody." Indeed they both had Captain de Sade's blood on them. "Kane!" He glanced over his shoulder at the little man with his same frown in place, but it was beginning to hide a growing respect for the Horotech. "Go outside and make sure that nag hasn't wandered off with our cart."

Laurence jumped when Geri barked out his name. He breathed a little easier when it became obvious that he wasn't going to be left behind, though he doubted very much that the brute was happy about it. Wisely not saying a word, Laurence nodded then quickly set to the task the Security Officer had given him. He cast up a prayer that this was the extent of the excitement they had on this mission. He wasn't certain his nerves could take any more.

VI
Excuse me, Mr. da Vinci

Geri had brought a canvas tarp from the hold when he and Nigel joined Laurence at the cart. They would use it to disguise the Gran Cavallo model when they procured it, but for now it would serve to hide the bloodstains. Laurence sat in the back on the tarp, unable to take his eyes from where the stain rested. It branded into his mind that this pirate business was serious. It wasn't just utilizing his skills to go back in time on whatever mission to retrieve whichever artifact as employment at Naviwerks would have been.

However, while the Corporation would have paid better, provided more personal security, and a better retirement package, Laurence was beginning to get a feeling in his gut that becoming a horological pirate was somehow morally superior. He had no proof, no actual clues as to why this might be, but his instincts had proven to be right a number of times before. Nigel seemed to be on his side as well. That counted for something. After all, the Historian was a learned man, and clever. Laurence looked at the two men sitting on the front bench of the cart and sighed quietly. He hoped his guts weren't just churning for the thought of what Dr. Hennessey was doing to poor Captain Alex.

It was a quiet trip back to Milan. Geri insisted on entering by another road which took them out of their way by an hour. Chance or the Security Officer's clever design put them on the eastern side of the very hill the shooter had used to sight on Captain Alex. There was no sign of the villain, of course, but that hadn't stopped Geri from looking for one anyway. Nigel made no comment of it. In fact, no one really spoke at all until they were approaching the guards at the gate.

Nigel reached into the back of the cart to place his hand on Laurence's shoulder, and with a small but encouraging smile told him he was up. The Horotech nodded as he recalled their original cover story. They were masquerading as representatives of a minor lord who wished to commission a piece from the artist Leonardo da Vinci.

They were delayed by the guards at the gate longer than they expected. There was some back and forth between Laurence and the guards that neither Nigel nor Geri could follow, but in the end the guards must have been satisfied because Laurence walked back to the cart, and they were waved through.

Once they were past the guards a smiling Nigel glanced back at Laurence. "Impressive, Mr. Kane. What did you say to them?"

"Ah . . . " Laurence's voice shook as he mopped beads of perspiration from his brow. "I gave them a name they would not argue with." He swallowed and hoped he hadn't overstepped his bounds with his spur of the moment improvisation.

Geri exchanged a glance with Nigel then spoke without turning around. His was the hand guiding the horse, and now that they were in the city proper he needed to not let the nag have her head. "What name did you give them?"

Laurence had to clear his throat before he murmured his reply. "The Borgias."

Geri straightened in his seat with a start when Nigel burst out laughing. His slender hands came together with a clap.

"What," Geri demanded from the Historian, a frown creasing his brows.

Nigel got his amusement contained down to chuckles as he placed a hand on Geri's shoulder in a reassuring gesture. "The Borgias were powerful, on again/off again popular, but primarily treacherous. Duke Sforza would not want to cross them even minutely and bring their attention to Milan. The guards would know this." He glanced back at Laurence again, and gave the Horotech a nod. "Well done, man."

Geri scowled even more. "Great. So the little twit may have just rewritten a little bit of history." They knew where da Vinci's studio was located, and Geri had the city map of this time memorized. He guided the horse off down a side street. "What's to say they won't try to follow up on what he told them? They find out he lied they'll come after us."

"Not a chance, old man." Nigel faced forward with a smug little smile on his face. "One does not claim an association with the Borgias lightly. If the authorities of Milan grow suspicious enough to look into the matter, most likely the Borgia family would be the offended parties, and come looking for us for explanations through painful methods." He shrugged nonchalantly. "By that time we will be long gone with our prize." He glanced back at Laurence again with that smile in place, and gave the nervous little man a wink. "No doubt our clever little Horotech knew this."

"Actually, it was them or Machiavelli, but I couldn't rightly remember if he was of the correct century." Laurence's confession brought another bark of laughter from the Historian.

Nigel had found the name of an inn not far from da Vinci's studio from looking at a traveler's map in his library of Milan, and given the directions to Geri. When they got there the Security Officer pulled the cart to a halt.

"Mr. Kane, you will have to be the one to hire a messenger to lure da Vinci from his studio." Nigel lifted his brows at Laurence. The little man would soon run out of tricks or courage in the Historian's opinion, but he wanted to give a visible show of confidence in the Horotech as a way to help keep Laurence motivated. "Do you remember what you planned to say?"

Laurence had to swallow before he nodded. "Yes." The smile he gave Nigel was more nervous than encouraging.

Nigel returned his smile with a more solid one. "Good man. Give whoever you hire a head start, then meet us at the studio."

"Provided the little twerp can find it." Geri's snide comment was given with a matching smirk.

Nigel sighed and resisted the urge to pinch the bridge of his nose. Instead he gave Geri a bland look as he pulled a pen out of a pocket inside his tunic. He held his hand out towards Laurence, and beckoned with his fingers. "Here. Give me your hand."

Laurence looked confused but did as he was told. Nigel turned his hand over and began drawing on the Horotech's palm. "Face down this street and follow the arrows." He finished quickly then nodded. "There." Geri got a pointed look from the Historian as if daring him to argue, and waste more time.

"Whatever." Geri huffed as he shook his head.

Laurence got out of the cart a few streets between the inn and da Vinci's studio, He looked more than a little lost standing there on his own with a forlorn expression on his face as he watched the cart round a corner and disappear from view. Geri didn't look back, but Nigel gave the Horotech an encouraging nod.

"At least he will not go terribly far off course if he gets lost," the Historian murmured to the Security Officer.

Geri grunted in return, "I ain't going to waste time hunting him down if we get the model."

Nigel said nothing until they had gotten to the street that housed da Vinci's studio, then waited until Geri had stopped the cart a couple of doors past before continuing the conversation. "Well, unless you can operate the chrono-engine we will have to."

He gave the Security Officer a lifted brow and knowing smirk that Geri didn't see. Nigel honestly believed in Laurence's capabilities having seen them in action. Thus far the little Horotech was proving to be valuable outside of the engine room. It would just take some time for Geri to accept that. Nigel knew this and was patient. He just hoped Laurence would be as well.

Long minutes passed by, and Nigel grew concerned that Laurence was unable to hire a messenger. Finally a young lad came jogging up to da Vinci's home and rapped on the door. Geri straightened in the cart which forced Nigel to move a little to see around the larger man. The boy knocked again, and after a moment the man himself came into partial view. Nigel gripped the back of the bench as he and Geri watched the exchange between the boy and the master artist. Laurence must have used the Borgia name again since da Vinci smoothed his hands over his garb nervously then gestured for the lad to lead the way. Both of them bustled off, hurriedly.

"Let's go." Geri's order was a quiet growl as he hopped down from the cart. Nigel slid to the ground a bit more gracefully, then stretched his legs to catch up with the taller Security Officer.

Both men knew that glancing around to see if anyone was watching would have been the quickest way to get caught. For Geri it was something he had been taught at officer academy. Nigel wouldn't say if you asked him, just replied with a smile and a wink. Regardless of the explanation, the two walked casually up to da Vinci's front door, and let themselves in.

The inside of da Vinci's home was sparse and orderly. Until they found their way into the artist's studio. There clutter abounded with parchment, brushes, drawing items, plates and other instruments lying around. It seemed a mess until one looked more closely and noticed that there was a sort of order to it all. Wood panels to be painted on were stacked in one section. Parchments in various state of use in another. Supplies yet another.

Just as Geri and Nigel were getting their bearings the front door burst open then was shut just as abruptly. They had long enough to look at each other before a breathless Laurence came into the studio.

"My apologies," he huffed out with his face flushed and blotchy. "I had to duck being seen by the boy I hired and who I can only assume was Mr. da Vinci." He bent over to put his hands on his knees in an effort to catch his breath.

Geri gave him a single scathing look before he returned to looking around the studio. Nigel smirked as he patted the exhausted Horotech on the shoulders. "Come on, dear boy. Help us find a four foot tall model of a horse." But the direction the Historian went off in proved to not be capable of containing a statue of that size. It did, however, contain sketches which he began poring through.

Laurence straightened with an almost pained look, but that changed into curiosity when he saw Nigel leafing through some parchment sheets. Excitement replaced that expression when he realized what the Historian was looking at, and he moved quickly to join him. "My God," he exclaimed quietly as he looked over Nigel's arm. "Those are…my God!"

Nigel chuckled quietly with a nod and an appreciative smile for the Horotech. "Anatomy sketches. He's already published one book that detailed the human body by this point, and is working on taking it to the next level. These would be the preliminary illustrations, if I do not miss my guess." Nigel knew that da Vinci's guesses at human anatomy had been more accurate than the official scholars' deductions that had followed for many centuries. His fascination with the sketches showed plainly on his face as he leafed through them.

Geri glowered back at them then frowned. "That's great, but it isn't a four foot bronze horse statue!" He gave the other two men a pointed glare. "Let's get on with it!" There wasn't much time, and he obviously wanted to be long on their way back to the ship before the artist caught on that he wasn't in fact meeting anyone at that inn.

Nigel rolled his eyes while Laurence looked guilty. "Oh, do calm down, man," Nigel said as he replaced the parchments reverently back where he had found them. "As if it will be difficult to miss the model. Although with your height you are liable to trip ov-.."

All three of them froze when they heard the front door open again. Geri's hand immediately went to the altered sword sheath that contained his plasma pistol. Nigel shook his head as he held up a hand in a wait gesture. Laurence just went pale, and seemed as if he might faint.

Muttering could be heard approaching the studio space. Nigel figured out what was happening first, and he reached out to grasp Laurence's shoulder.

He hauled the Horotech to him, and spoke in a harsh whisper. "It appears we will have to rely on your quick wit one more time, Mr. Kane. Look sharp now." And just as Leonardo da Vinci himself came into his studio Nigel gave Laurence a small shake, and the Horotech stumbled forward.

The Historian wore a calm smile when da Vinci looked up in surprise to see people in his home. Laurence straightened himself, and smoothed a hand over his tunic as he wiped a panicked look from his face. Meanwhile, Geri lurked behind the door prepared to knock the artist out if need be.

"W-what is this?" da Vinci asked in Italian with a quiet voice. He looked over all three men, but finally settled on Laurence since he was in front. *"I do not believe I was expecting guests."*

A few awkward moments passed in silence as the crew members collectively breathed a sigh of relief, then Nigel prodded Laurence in the kidney with a finger. The Horotech startled, then addressed *the* Leonardo da Vinci.

"No, sir. You were not." Laurence was proud to hear that he wasn't stammering, but he knew he would have to sound much more confident in order to pull this off. He said a silent prayer and continued. *"I ah…we… have come representing our lord and master who wishes to commission a piece from you."*

The archaic Italian seemed a little sketchy to Laurence's ears, and it was quite possible that he was making a mess of it by the confused look that remained on da Vinci's face. It was also nerve-wracking to translate the conversation for Geri and Nigel as the artist spoke.

"What lord is that, sir?" But before Laurence could answer da Vinci's question the artist's face screwed up into a grimace, and he waved it off with

a broad gesture of his stained fingers. *"Later. Come back later, good gentlemen. I must be about some business first then perhaps we can discuss this commission."* He bustled further into the studio, pushed gently past Laurence as he moved to a desk where he began searching through the items stacked there as he muttered *"I would forget my own head if it were not attached, let alone sketches."*. He obviously expected them to just leave as instructed.

Laurence turned a helpless look to Nigel as he translated. The Historian widened his eyes at the Horotech. He waved his hands at Laurence to encourage him to continue. The smaller man swallowed before he turned back to the artist. *"Your pardon, sir, but we are that business you were about."*

Da Vinci turned with brows lifted to look at Laurence in growing confusion. *"But we were to meet at the inn. The boy said."*

Laurence gave him a nervous smile. *"Yes, my apologies. We thought it better to meet with you in your studio. I had hoped to arrive before my message, but we were delayed. We waited for your return."* Dear God, he was no good at lying!

Da Vinci was obviously growing suspicious as he eyed the young man speaking to him. *"Who did you say your lord was, sir?"*

Laurence at least felt confident enough to answer this with surety. *"Borgia, sir."*

"Which one?" came da Vinci's challenging question quickly.

"Which one?" The question caught Laurence off guard. It shouldn't have, but there it was. So much for his confidence. Laurence wasn't prepared to get that detailed in his lie, and now he was left flat footed.

Nigel came instantly to his rescue. His voice was next to Laurence's ear. *"Cesare."*

"Cesare!" blurted the nervous Horotech.

"Ah!" Apparently da Vinci didn't notice the little verbal slip. The artist smiled. *"The cardinal's son, yes? Yes, yes. Well met then, my lords."* He waved for them as if gesturing them into the studio they were already standing in. *"Come. Tell me of this commission. I can show you samples of what I have already accomplished, and what I am currently working on."* He bustled towards another desk where he pulled out some more parchments. *"Look you. See? Sketches for Annunciation to the Virgin. Old, though. Not a style I work in now. But this!"* He turned to wave a parchment in Mr. Kane's direction. *"Madonna of the Rocks. A good example. Well, moderate."*

Laurence made a show of looking at the sketches. To be honest, he didn't have to stretch his performance much. How often was it that one was able to see sketches by Leonardo da Vinci just years after the man had drawn them?

Geri cleared his throat, bringing Laurence back to the task at hand, and the Horotech gave the artist what he hoped was a placating smile. It looked more like he was about to get sick, most likely. *"All very nice, my good man, but my lord had something else in mind. A statue. Word had reached him that Duke Sforza had commissioned you for a horse statue of impressive size."*

"Ah! Yes!" Da Vinci wagged a finger in the

air with a proud smile on his face before he turned to a set of shelves attached to the wall beside the desk. He pulled down a few sheets of parchment reverently to spread them on the desk. *"Look. My preliminary sketches."* Indeed, each piece of parchment was a study of some different part of a muscular horse, and rather impressive at that. *"It shall be bronze. The Gran Cavallo is what I shall call it."* He held one arm out, and shook it just slightly, enough to get attention. *"Twenty four times the length of my arm from wrist to elbow! That is how tall it shall be."*

It took Laurence a moment to remember that they did not have specific units of measurement in the fifteenth century so the artist had been explaining that the statue would be twenty four feet tall. He smiled as he nodded. *"Very impressive, sir. Have you worked up any models of the statue? Trial attempts, as it were."*

"Yes." Geri was suddenly paying more attention after Laurence translated that, but da Vinci's expression fell into something between disappointment and annoyance. *"I would have liked to show it to you, but it was taken just two days ago."*

Hearing that translated, Nigel blinked in surprise. The model wasn't supposed to have gone missing for another nine years! He exchanged a look with Geri who cursed in a hushed tone. The Historian turned his attention back to Laurence and nodded to him. "Ask him who took it, Mr. Kane."

Laurence did as he was instructed with a sympathetic smile for da Vinci. *"Taken! How shocking. By whom?"*

The artist nodded with a heavy sigh, and his

scowl brought his brows down over his eyes. *"Indeed. They said they were in the employ of the Pope, and that His Holiness sent them to retrieve the model. I cannot understand why He would want it. I alerted the guard to the theft. They assured me that they would strengthen the watch at the gates since they had been garbed in no livery of the Holy See that I had ever seen."* He waved a hand in the air over his head as if he were trying to shoo the culprits out now.

Geri let out with another curse, this time not quite so hushed, and began to pace. That explained the delay they'd had with the guards at the gate. This was very bad news. How they were going to explain to the Captain that the model had already been taken was anyone's guess. Failure was not something that anyone on the crew took lightly.

"Ask him to describe them." That had been far less of a request from Geri, and more of a command.

Da Vinci looked to the large man with a growing interest. *"You must be emissaries or ambassadors from the north, if I am correct in guessing that language."* He looked back to the young man who spoke his own tongue. *"English, yes?"*

Laurence felt like scrubbing his hand over his face, as his nerves jumped continuously. Instead he gave the artist a tight smile, and skipped past the question. He doubted very much that he could continue with the ruse if he had to make up much more. *"Could you describe these scoundrels? It might be that they are adversaries of our lord and master. He would know if someone is meddling in his affairs."*

Da Vinci eyed the three of them for a quiet moment, and noted that the larger man was visibly growing impatient. The artist was technically in the employ of Duke Sforza. Laurence thought he would not want to involve himself in any political maneuvering even obliquely. Still, the Borgias were not a family one wanted to annoy so finally da Vinci shrugged before he answered. *"Five men. No six. One was obviously their captain or some such authority rank. Fine garments of yellow and blue."*

After Laurence translated Nigel frowned deeply, and turned to pace away, deeply troubled. This made no sense to Nigel. The Corporation never did anything without a reason, and they certainly never threatened historical time lines.

Meanwhile, Geri was clenching his jaw as he snarled at Laurence "Ask him to describe the one in charge." The Security Officer once held rank in the guard for Naviwerks. He knew quite a few of the Agents, and might recognize whichever one had been to see da Vinci.

Laurence dutifully turned back to da Vinci, and conveyed the Security Officer's question. The master artist nodded as he held his hand up a bit, a finger pointed at Nigel's back. *"Almost as tall as that gentleman there. Dark blue eyes that seemed rather piercing and fierce. His hair was covered by a helm, but he had a scar,"* he drew a finger from his cheekbone forward and down to just above his jaw line, *"just here. Faint. A long time healed. Neatly, at that."*

Laurence translated the description, and immediately Geri sneered. "Nash!" He spat to the side with his fists clenched.

Nigel whirled around with a stunned look at Geri. His lips parted slightly and he blinked. "Oh dear." This couldn't have been more awkward.

Laurence and da Vinci both wore confused expressions. "What. Who is Nash?" Laurence asked quietly of Nigel.

Nigel began to answer. "Agent Nash and Captain de Sade-"

"Worked together." Geri's interruption was firm, and he gave Nigel a pointed look. "For most of her time at Naviwerks as Captain" Geri stared Nigel in the eyes as he made a silent point. Some things were not theirs to tell. "And it looks like he just tried to kill her."

In Irons

VII
Who is Agent Nash?

Nigel let out with a quiet sigh as he nodded to Geri then turned to pace away. Laurence Kane would have bet his chrono-engine repair kits that he never would have witnessed Nigel Wellington behave awkwardly, yet he was seeing it now. He watched the Historian but knew he would have to turn his attention back to da Vinci soon. "I see." He felt there was far more to this story than just Agent Nash and Captain Alex having worked together. With this information, however, he couldn't help but wonder how their injured Captain was going to receive these facts. Not only was their contracted target gone, but that it had been a once trusted business partner that had tried to assassinate her.

Geri Reynolds kept a suspicious eye on Nigel. The Security Officer was obviously fuming mad. His jaw muscles kept tightening almost as if he were gnashing his teeth repeatedly. Laurence had already been feeling tense, and it had been mounting ever since Captain de Sade had been shot. But the pressure had multiplied even more with the confirmation of the identity of Agent Nash as the potential shooter. The Horotech cast a worried look from Geri to Nigel. "So what do we do now?"

"We get back to the ship." Geri's answer was stern. "Ain't nothing here for us now, and we have to report in."

Nigel turned around to look at Geri. Laurence thought *he* was typically an open book, but right now Nigel was putting him to shame. The Historian looked more disappointed than worried, though that was there too. With another sigh Nigel nodded to Geri. "Yes, you are probably right." He sounded more resigned than the confident leader he had been up until this point.

Da Vinci had been listening to all of this, and wasn't understanding a word judging by the blank look on his face. Laurence gave the artist a polite smile when he turned back to him. *"Thank you for your time, but it seems that we must consult with our Lord Borgia for further instructions,"* he said in fifteenth century Italian. Then he was suddenly being pulled towards the door by an impatient Geri. Laurence stumbled a little as he lifted a hand towards da Vinci. *"We will be in touch."* Then he grumbled under his breath at Geri. "I say! Let go of me."

Da Vinci just lifted his hand in a hesitant wave in return, and looked a little stunned as the three men left his studio.

Geri had shot Laurence a stern look that kept the smaller man from batting at the Security Officer's hand. Fortunately, Geri released him as soon as they were in the street. Laurence stopped to catch his breath as the larger man made for the cart with determined steps. Nigel stopped next to the Horotech and put his hand on the shorter man's shoulder. "Come on. Even with a chrono-ship, time and bad news wait for no man."

Laurence looked up at Nigel. It dawned on him at that moment that ever since he had met the Historian on the dock outside of the warehouse that *The William's Hunt* made berth in, he had been the most encouraging member of the crew to Laurence. It pulled a small smile from the Horotech, and he nodded. "Yes, of course."

Nigel patted his shoulder then followed after Geri before the Security Officer decided to leave with or without them. Laurence was a step behind.

Nigel chose to sit next to the Security Officer on the bench in the front of the cart while Laurence occupied the back. None of them said anything as they left Milan, and the silence wasn't broken until they were well on their way down the road.

Laurence's mind had been turning on Geri and Nigel's reactions to the positive identification of Agent Nash. He knew he would get no more details from either of them on the subject of the Agent and Captain Alex, but he would like to learn more about the Agent in general. He moved himself closer to the back of the bench and cleared his throat. "This Agent Nash. It seems you both know him." He saw Geri's shoulders tense up, and Nigel's face went blank. "What manner of person is he?"

Nigel turned that look to Geri, and lifted his brows as if in silent question. "It's a fair question." Geri slid a disapproving glance at Nigel who spread his hands. “In for a pound, my friend. If we are going to be facing him, the lad deserves to know what to expect.”

“Whatever.” Geri’s voice was a growl as he faced forward again and gave the horse a twitch of the reins. He didn’t say anything however which left Nigel to begin.

“I never worked with him,” Nigel said as he looked back to Laurence. “Thank God.”

That surprised Laurence, but he was relieved that the two men were willing to talk on the subject even if reluctantly. “Why thank God?”

Nigel draped his elbow over the back of the bench after pushing his fingers through his mess of loose curls. “He has a reputation for being a bit harsh. Cold even. I wouldn’t say he was ruthless,” he stopped himself for a moment as he pressed his lips together. “Well. I wouldn’t have before today, anyway, but even before he decided to take a cheap shot at our dear Captain he was intimidating to most everyone unless you were a member of his security team.” Now he slid a glance to Geri that to Laurence seemed a little pointed.

“He is ruthless.” Geri’s tone was harsh, disapproving. “Always has been. Always will be.”

Laurence had looked at Geri’s broad shoulders then exchanged a look with Nigel before he adjusted his position in the back of the cart to get a better view of the Security Officer. “You worked with him.” It was less of a question and more of a statement which he hoped would encourage Geri to continue.

The large man nodded exactly once. “I was a member of the security pool he would draw from before I was assigned to Captain Alex’s ship. Nash was Tier

4 then. Those are the Agents that get sent out with the ships to ensure that Naviwerks' will is done." Geri was all but sneering now. "Nash would take a security squad with him. Wasn't typical. He wanted us to linger around with the crew. Listen in on what they were saying. Spies, basically. Didn't feel right to me so I kept my head down and my mouth shut, but there was a few times things got reported and Nash went to the next level of exiling folk in the past." This time when he paused he spat off the side of the cart again. "After seeing that happen just once I made sure I was elsewhere when he came looking to form a squad. Didn't see him again until he was Tier 3 and I was assigned permanent on Captain Alex's boat."

"What's the difference between Tier 3 and Tier 4?" Laurence had never worked for Naviwerks so he wasn't familiar with their protocols.

"Tier 4 Agents are the field officers," Nigel answered.. "Tier 3's are commanders. Typically they work out of an office at the Corporation, and assign the lower ranked Agents that they are in charge of."

"Typically?" asked Laurence.

"Wasn't Nash's way to sit behind a desk." Geri picked up the explanations again. For as hesitant to speak about the Agent as he had been he seemed amiable enough now. If angry. "He just took the power he was given and put himself where he wanted to be. Right on the Captain's ship." He said that all through clenched teeth which made Nigel look at him in concern. "I was already assigned or he might have picked me, but he decided to form a new squad of enforcers within Naviwerks' security department. Answered only to him and he set them on other ships anytime there was a report of a…an undesirable attitude." Geri's sarcasm like a natural talent. "The disappearances increased after that, but they were quiet. They said folk retired, or found job opportunities elsewhere. Most of us knew better."

A look was shared between Nigel and Geri before the Security Officer faced the road again. Laurence wasn't sure what inner knowledge the two had, but it was obvious that it made Nigel sad and Geri frustrated. "And now he's after us?" With his own personal death squad, and security guards, *and* any other Agents he cared to enlist if Laurence understood this correctly.

"It certainly looks that way." Nigel gave Laurence a helpless smile and a shrug, but the Horotech caught the hint of worry in the Historian's pale brown eyes.

"Captain de Sade isn't going to let this deter her, is she?" There had already been one near argument with the wounded Captain about whether to continue with the mission. She had won. Laurence couldn't see that stubborn woman backing off just because a man with a small army and an intimidating reputation was hunting her and her crew.

"No reason why she should." Geri had a note of determination in his voice when he answered that. "Captain put this crew together on a stolen boat to go up against the Corporation, and Nash stands for everything they do that's wrong." He finally glanced over his shoulder at Laurence. The smirk on his face wasn't meant to be comforting, neither was the waggle of his eyebrows. "Besides. We ain't exactly defenseless."

That might have been the friendliest Geri Reynolds had ever been to Laurence. It surprised the smaller Horotech for a moment before the words finally sank in. Laurence blinked a couple of times in confusion. "What…what do you mean? I know you have weapons, but you both are suggesting that Agent Nash could quite possibly come gunning for us with half an army that is well paid and well trained by Naviwerks."

This time when Geri and Nigel exchanged a look it was more smug than concerned. Geri faced forward again, and Laurence could have sworn the man was grinning. "Don't worry about it." He gave a shrill whistle to the horse as he twitched its hind end with the reins again. "You just keep those engines working right."

Nigel rolled his eyes a little before he turned a smirk back to Laurence. "What he means to say is that nobody wants to go up against Agent Nash unprepared. Not even our hulking friend here." Geri grumbled at Nigel when the Historian nudged him. "And this was not entirely unexpected. Perhaps just not so directly out of the gate."

Laurence looked at Nigel as if he thought the Historian was off his nut. His eyes went to Geri's wide back briefly before he settled down again in the back of the cart. "I see." He tried not to take the quiet chuckle from Nigel too personally.

He might have thought that the ease with which the Historian returned to a jovial mood might seem odd after the show of concern he'd had just moments ago, except that Laurence had taken note that not once had the Historian's amusement been expressed beyond his lips. Maybe they had expected Naviwerks to come after them, especially since Captain Alex had stolen one of their chrono-ships. Maybe they hadn't expected the Corporation's retaliation to have happened so soon. And it certainly was concerning that their first contract attempt had been discovered and thwarted. But Geri and Nigel seemed to adjust to these surprises quickly, and Laurence had no doubt that Angel, Dr. Hennessey and Captain Alex would be the same way. He sighed then muttered into his hand before it pushed back through his hair. "They are all either very clever or incredibly insane." He wasn't certain which would make him more nervous.

Back in the medical bay of *The William's Hunt* Dr. Hennessey had finished stitching up Captain Alex's plasma shot wounds. He had her resting comfortably on the multi-purposed exam table where he insisted that she remain so he could keep an eye on her vitals. She was doped up just enough to make her compliant with that request, but not so much that she wasn't cranky about the whole thing. She kept giving the Doctor annoyed looks which he ignored easily through long experience with irritable patients, Captain Alex included.

"Glare all you want, my dear," Dr. Hennessey said as he put a tray of instruments into the autoclave, then began setting the dials for the sterilization run. "Here you will stay until I am certain you aren't going to tear open those stitches through some foolishness or another."

Alex rolled her eyes as she let out with a petulant sigh. Only the Doctor could make her feel as if she were twelve years old instead of thirty two. "I have a ship to run, Abraham." Her speech was a little slurred from the pain medication. Hearing it made her even more frustrated. "And an away team to check on. I don't have time to be a lubber in your medical bay."

Dr. Hennessey turned around with a steely look for Captain Alex. "Need I remind you of our agreement?"

But before either of them could continue Angel Flynn's voice came out through the ship's internal comm speaker. *"Away team returning, Captain."*

Captain Alex knew better than to sit up let alone try to get off the exam table, but she did point a wobbly finger at Dr. Hennessey in warning. The huff he gave in reply made his mutton chop sideburns wriggle as he flipped the switch on the comm unit to voice activation then crossed his arms stubbornly. Alex lowered her hand with more of a flop than a controlled movement. This was her ship, damn it, and she would be Captain to her crew with or without injuries. "Do they have the statue, Miss Flynn?"

"That's a negative, Cap," came Angel's flippant reply. *"No horsy and Mr. Reynolds looks ready to spit more than usual."*

Alex's pale blue eyes landed solidly on Dr. Hennessey. Something had gone wrong to make Geri abandon the mission. There was plenty of time left before the wormhole sealed leaving them unable to return to their own time period. Angel hadn't said any of them were injured so it couldn't have been that they ran into the shooter or any friends he might have had with him. So what made someone as dedicated as her Security Officer return empty handed?

"I need to receive their report, Doctor." Alex went back to being formal with Dr. Hennessey now that someone else was listening to their conversation. She and the Doctor had known each other a long time, almost her whole life, but her dignity wouldn't allow that familiarity to show through in case it was seen as favoritism. Not that anyone in her crew would accuse her of that, but it was a habit she had made a point of developing during her time with Naviwerks.

"You need to be still, and let the fast track meds I shot you up with do their work." Dr. Hennessey wagged a thick finger at his patient, one bushy eyebrow arching upwards.

"Then I will meet with them here." Alex did her best to be firm, but it came out like more of a whine than she cared for. She clenched her teeth together for a moment before she let Dr. Hennessey see a bit more of how she was feeling than she would ever show to anyone. She was determined almost to the point of desperation, and yes, frightened to a degree. "Please."

Whichever part it was that the Doctor saw on the tiny Captain's expression that swayed him Alex might never know, but he screwed up his face into a disapproving frown and harrumphed again. "Fine." He pointed his finger at her again. "But do not ask me for another pain shot if you burn through what is in your system already."

"Agreed." Alex smiled at him in gratitude then raised her voice as well as she could. "Have them report to the medical bay, Miss Flynn."

"Aye, Cap." Dr. Hennessey and Captain Alex could hear the click through the speaker that meant

Angel had disengaged the internal comm after she responded.

Alex looked up at Dr. Hennessey in silence for a few moments. His suspicious expression let her know that her attempt at giving him a thankful look wasn't fooling him one bit. He was proven correct when she opened her mouth. "I suppose it might be too much to ask that you give me a boost with something that might clear my head some for this."

"Damn right!" The Doctor gave Captain Alex a sharp look even as he placed his foot on a pedal under the exam table and began manipulating toggles. The table gave the slightest of jerks as hydraulic pistons expanded to fold the upper portion so that the Captain was more in a reclining sit rather than lying down. A pull of a lever locked the gears in place once the Doctor was satisfied with the table's position.

It was as much of a concession as he was going to give and Alex knew it. She placed her hand on Dr. Hennessey's arm, and gave him a smile in thanks. He let out with a muted *hmph* as he patted her hand then returned to cleaning his instruments.

Soon after the rest of her crew walked into the exam room. Each of them wore a different expression of trepidation. With the exception of Angel who didn't hesitate to sit on a counter top, and Dr. Hennessey who tried unsuccessfully to stop her, the expressions changed from anxious to surprise or embarrassment. Angel had fetched a clean grey tank top for Captain Alex to put on after she was done having her injuries tended to, but for comfort sake Angel had only brought a pair of thermal pants instead of the Captain's uniform pants. To the men of her crew who didn't work in the medical field however she might as well be wandering around the ship in her never-you-minds. Worst of all, she was barefoot.

Alex arched a brow as she watched them mentally back peddle in order to deal with her state of dress. Laurence turned beet red as he averted his eyes to the side, to the ceiling, the floor, anywhere but at her. Geri lowered his entire face with his hands clasped behind his back as he cleared his throat. As for Nigel, Alex knew that the only reason his face was turning red was from trying to keep from laughing and was not entirely successful judging by how his shoulders hitched from time to time.

"Well?" she asked and was relieved to hear her voice be close to its usual strength.

Awkwardness remained but for an entirely different reason now. Alex picked up on the shift easily, but she waited patiently as the three men collected themselves. It was Nigel who stepped towards her and began to give a report. She would have bet Geri to be the one, and was surprised when it wasn't. Some part of her grew just as anxious as her crew seemed to be for that alone. Not much intimidated the large Security Officer.

"We met with Leonardo da Vinci." Nigel came to stand next to Captain Alex's ankles which would allow her to see everyone with little difficulty. She appreciated that, and listened to Nigel without interrupting him. Meeting with the artist had never been in the plans, but she would hear him out.

"The man returned to his studio before we had a

chance to adequately search for the Gran Cavallo model." Nigel laced his fingers together at his waist as he spoke. Alex recognized his posture as the same one he adopted when he used to give lectures as a Historian for Naviwerks. "As it turned out this was fortuitous since the model was not there. We learned from da Vinci that it had been confiscated just two days ago." Nigel paused. Alex could tell that it was not for dramatic effect which would not be out of the realm of expectation when it came to her Historian. Nigel was honestly hesitant about something. "By members of the Papal Swiss Guard."

Captain Alex frowned in confusion. She opened her mouth to say that was impossible, but recalled that she had promised herself not to interrupt Nigel. Besides, she could tell that this paradox was not what had Nigel, Geri, and Laurence so concerned. There was something more to this. She would know what that was so she just looked expectantly at Nigel as she pressed her lips together.

The Historian looked his Captain in the eyes, pale brown to pale blue and spoke gently. "He described the captain of the troop that took the statue. It was Agent Nash."

A series of emotions shot through Alex upon hearing that name. Her eyes widened fractionally and went hard. Her blood first turned to ice before becoming like lava flowing through her veins. It was as if that name had the ability to separate her mind from the meds Dr. Hennessey had shot into her since it was suddenly working flint sharp. She wasn't even aware that her left hand had clenched into a tight fist, nor that her breathing and her heart beat had sped up.

Nash. She had expected to run into him at some point. Her chosen profession made that inevitable since she was practically daring him to come after her for stealing the chrono-ship from Naviwerks when she left their employment. Alex told herself she shouldn't be surprised that he was that quick about it. She also told herself that she didn't care beyond the fact that he was a dangerous man to cross. The first part wasn't as easy to accept as the latter, but there was no way she would allow her crew to see these reactions let alone admit them openly.

Geri cleared his throat which brought Alex's attention to him. "It's probably safe to assume he's the one that…was on the hill. This morning." His hesitation was obvious. He had been about to say something else. Alex wasn't entirely sure what he kept behind his teeth, but it didn't really matter.

"Thank you, Mr. Reynolds." The Captain's voice had gone tight and flat. "I share that opinion." And it wasn't lost on her what that meant. Not by half. Her eyes looked over the faces of her crew individually, and she could tell that they all knew too. Save for Laurence Kane. The Horotech hadn't known any of them before a few hours ago when he reported for duty. If the rest of them knew what was good for them they would keep their mouths shut about it, or find themselves cleaning the hull of the ship every day for the next month.

"Do we know where they took the model?" Her question drew different reactions from each of them. Dr. Hennessey sighed before running his hand over his face. Laurence looked conflicted. Angel dared to smirk a little along with Nigel, and Geri just looked more disapproving than usual.

"Da Vinci said they were taking it to the Pope," said Geri. "Could be they were telling the truth. Could be the model's already gone back. Loaded on a Naviwerks ship."

"Your opinion?" Alex knew that her Security Officer had worked with Nash before. If any of them besides her knew how Nash worked it would be Geri Reynolds.

"Don't have enough intel, Captain." Geri now looked uncomfortable as well as grouchy.

Alex's slender brows came down. She had no patience for perfection at the moment. "Your best guess will do, Mr. Reynolds." His guesses were better than most people's facts in these circumstances.

"They're both still here," Geri said in an almost resigned tone. "The model and Nash."

"Reasoning?" came Alex's immediate challenge

"Nash is thorough." Now that Captain Alex had him talking Geri was getting less awkward. His face lifted entirely, and he crossed his arms over his chest. "That weren't no warning shot. He would have followed up looking for verification of the kill. When he didn't find one, and assuming he knows we're after the Gran Cavallo, he'd use it as bait. Draw you back out."

There was more to it than that. This would be personal to Nash, and Alex knew it. If for no other reason than that, Nash would stick around. "They *hope* we will follow after them for the model." Alex's eyes narrowed in thought. There were plenty of options.

None of them she liked.

"Recommendations?" She phrased it that way to indicate that any of them were welcome to speak up.

"Wait until full night." Geri opted to go first. Knowing him as well as she did, Captain Alex could see that what the Security Officer was recommending was not his first choice, but he knew her well too. Alex wasn't going to give up on this. "Fly dark. Locate their camp. If it is bait, the model will be easy to find."

Angel spoke up from where she sat on the counter. "Not only can I run her dark, Cap, but first sight of a camp and I can run her silent." At the questioning look Captain Alex gave her Angel smirked. "The William'll coast as good as a kite if I need her to. There's no ambient noise here in the back end of progress, but there's plenty of wind. No sense alerting them to our presence if we're trying to be sneaky."

"Send in a small group, armed." Nigel brought their Captain's attention back to him. "To the teeth would be preferable. A four foot bronze statue will be an awkward swag to move with any sort of stealth, but it is possible. I would still be more comfortable knowing you are nearby to pick us up once we have it."

"A touch and go pick up is easy," Angel assured him.

Captain Alex looked over to Dr. Hennessey without a nod or any other indication of her opinion thus far, but the Doctor held his hands up and shook his head. "Don't look at me. I have a mind for medicine not tactics." He grumbled out some nonsense when Alex gave him a flat look of disbelief. "I might have something to knock a man senseless if you're close enough to deliver a hypo-spray. *Might.*" Dr. Hennessey shook a finger at Geri. "I'm trusting you lot to not abuse it."

Geri smirked back at the Doctor. "Think you could rig that into something what could be fired from a rifle, Doc?"

"That's enough." Captain Alex decided to shut that bickering down in the birthing. She knew full well they could go round and round about something like that, Geri and Dr. Hennessey. Her Security Officer might have come across as simply baiting the Doctor, but Alex knew he would love ammunition such as he described, and Dr. Hennessey would be adamantly against it.

"Mr. Kane." Alex turned her attention on Laurence who startled visibly to suddenly be addressed. "We have yet to hear from you."

"Oh." Laurence flickered a nervous glance from one crew member to the other, anyone but Captain Alex. She found that amusing but kept that thought to herself and off of her face. "Well." He cleared his throat either in an obvious bid to buy some time, or from habit. Either was a fair bet. "Do we have any uniforms of the Papal Guard?"

Alex thought she saw where the Horotech was going with this. A glance to Nigel told her that he did too. The covert smile on his face and wink he gave her made her curious to know what has happened between the away team while they were in Milan. She made a mental note to speak at length with her Historian when this was all over.

For now she looked to Geri who was more than passing familiar with the contents of the hold of the ship. “Mr. Reynolds?”

Geri shook his head. “Don’t remember seeing any available to snitch when I got the rest of the wardrobes.” Which made him frown to think about. Naviwerks had access to costumes and clothing of any era in time. Their Historians worked very closely with their Garment Department to get things period perfect. He exchanged a meaningful stare with Captain Alex who gave a small nod to indicate that she was thinking the same thing.

“What are your thoughts, Mr. Kane?” Alex turned the attention back to the small Horotech who looked as if she had turned a spotlight on him.

Laurence scratched at the side of his nose as he began then pushed his spectacles up a bit higher on the bridge of his nose. “It seems to me as if this should be a clandestine infiltration sort of mission at this point, and what better way to go unnoticed than to blend in.” What little confidence had been present on his face fled when he noticed the scrutiny turned on him by Geri. He edged away from the Security Officer a little as he continued. “Mr. Reynolds might be all too easily recognized regardless of costume since he has worked with Agent Nash before, and his uh…size makes him stand out. As I understand it, Mr. Wellington has never worked directly with the Agent and I have never worked for Naviwerks at all.” He swallowed when Geri gave him a very disapproving look and stepped towards him. “So I propose that Mr. Wellington and I be the extent of the team to enter the camp, but it is a moot point since we haven’t any uniforms.”

Captain Alex was quiet for a few moments

as she thought that over. It wasn't a bad idea, but she didn't think Laurence was ready for something quite that involved. Still, while she wasn't a harsh task master she was not above tossing someone into the drink to make them sink or swim. Laurence would have to toughen up if he was going to fly with them. She believed he had it in him so she would encourage this plan, but she had an alteration for it. "We haven't any uniforms *yet*."

She held up a hand to keep Geri from interrupting her. It was backed up with as stern of a look as she could drum up under the influence of the meds she had been given. "We wait here until after sunset. Angel will take us up running dark." Captain Alex turned her head to look at her Pilot. "Extend the visuals as far as they will go. First sign of life go dead in the air. I want to see if she'll drift as far as you say she can."

When she turned back to Geri, Nigel and Laurence she pointed a finger, but at none of them in particular. She didn't want to single any one out. "You three get out of those clothes and into something more concealing. Arm yourself." Alex arched an auburn brow at her Security Officer. "Including Mr. Kane, and I want you to break out the box, Mr. Reynolds."

Captain Alex was satisfied to see her instructions put a grim looking smile on Geri's face. She nodded her approval before she continued. "Take the comms. I want you in constant contact with Miss Flynn who will be scrambling the signal in case they are monitoring frequencies. I want it to sound like crickets to anyone but us."

"Aye, Cap," came Angel's eager reply.

Alex waited until Angel had slipped out of the room then addressed the three men again. "Mr. Reynolds is in charge of this. I want that understood. Get up to the camp and get into some uniforms. Avoid Agent Nash at *all* costs. Abandon the swag if you have to." Her cold blue eyes went to Geri and stayed there. "Eliminate him if he gets in the way." The tension in the room increased threefold at her words, but no one dared say anything. Alex didn't release her Security Officer from her stare until he nodded in agreement. "Get to it, then."

Alex relaxed against the exam table as Laurence and Geri turned to leave, but she nudged Nigel with her foot when he made to follow them. He lingered with a curious look on his face. She let a little more of her concern show through. Not as much as she had shown Dr. Hennessey earlier, but Nigel wouldn't betray her trust in him with her openness. "Keep an eye on them. Don't let Geri step all over Kane's attempts."

Nigel gave Captain Alex a gentle smile as he covered her hand with his. "Rest assured, my dear Captain. I am well ahead of you with them." He chuckled as she frowned when he patted her hand. "They will be fine."

Captain Alex huffed as she pulled her hand out from under Nigel's only to flap it at him in a shooing gesture. "Go." She couldn't help but smirk when her Historian gave her another wink before following after Geri and Laurence.

Another hand came to rest on her shoulder after Nigel had left. Alex rested back entirely in the chair and looked up at Dr. Hennessey. He wore a more caring expression on his face this time instead of the constant disapproving look he typically wore. "I am glad that you were shot."

"Excuse me?" Alex practically sputtered to hear that, and her slender eyebrows shot straight up on her forehead. Of all of the things that the Doctor might say to her *that* was the last thing she thought she would hear from him.

"I am not prepared to patch you up as I did the last time you saw him, Alexandria." Only Dr. Hennessey was allowed to call her by her full name, and it affected Alex the way it always did, especially when he used that gentle tone of voice. She lowered her eyes to her left hand where it rested on the exam table. Just looking at it made her fingers curl inward.

"I don't think I'm ready for that either, Abraham."

VIII
Infiltration

The pirate chrono-ship *The William's Hunt* flew high in the fifteenth century Italian night. The only lights were on the bridge from the flight controls of the helm and the visual display ship's Pilot Angel Flynn was using to navigate by. The same steam that ran the turbines to create the ship's electricity was released between pressed glass, and an image of the darkened Italian countryside was projected upon it. The visual range was pushed to the limit so that Angel would have enough warning to cut the engines and coast once a camp was spotted.

Running dark was not just easy, but necessary when spending five days in the past. Not many captains made use of the chrono-ships' flight ability, but there were some very specific instructions that were to be followed to avoid paradox should they choose to do so. Fly dark, fly high, fly silent. They weren't always successful. That was when strange objects would show up in the skies of paintings, or were recorded in documents. More often than not the sightings were chalked up as meteors since the chrono-ships' contrails evaporated quickly thanks in part to the chemical compound the engines burned. The fuel burned clean since it didn't ignite until it was heated to steam form. The process also made the fuel last longer than a liquid equivalent.

Geri, Nigel and Laurence were on the bridge with Angel dressed for their mission in tight fitted matte black clothing. Laurence shifted and tugged at the garment uncomfortably which amused Nigel. Geri ignored them both in lieu of watching the display. All three men were armed with pistols that were loaded with plasma rounds and nightsticks, but the Security Officer had additions to his arsenal. The gun with the knock out shot that Dr. Hennessey had given him was in a holster designed for it tied to his belt and secured against his thigh with a dull black leather strap. But it was the rifle slung over his shoulder that one noticed first. Laurence had when they had been gearing up in the hold. Geri smirked to himself as he thought about the Horotech's reaction.

"Isn't that a bit ah...conspicuous?" asked Laurence as he watched Geri check the barrel of the rifle he had retrieved from the weapons cache in the hold of the ship where the three of them were preparing for their undercover task.

Geri gave the Horotech a withering look as he snapped the bolt back in place then slung the rifle over his shoulder. "Very. But dimes to dollars we'll need it." His smirk was smug if a bit dark as he pulled out an unmarked box of bullets. After opening it he began to load the rounds into the rifle.

Nigel's brows lifted as he took note of the bullets. "I thought those hadn't been officially tested."

"No time like the present," said Geri without looking up from his task.

"What?" Laurence looked as if he were finally reconsidering this whole adventure as he looked from Geri to Nigel. "Untested? What manner of bullets are they?"

"They didn't have a name yet." The Historian took a step towards Laurence as if he wanted some space between himself and Geri. "Because they never made it past a beta test. Naviwerks' engineers referred to them as chrono-rounds. Essentially they are plasma rounds loaded with the same chemicals that operate the chrono-engines. Expectations were that the chemicals combined with gunpowder would ignite upon impact with a target and set off the same reaction that creates the wormholes. The victim would be frozen in time for a space of five minutes to five hours."

Laurence as a Horotech and in charge of operating and maintaining the chrono-engine clearly understood the difficulties inherent in creating such a weapon, but was far too aghast at the idea of turning a chrono-engine into a weapon at all. He stared at the Historian with that expression on his face. "Good Lord!" He swallowed convulsively. "What happened during testing?"

Nigel sighed as he gave Geri a disapproving look. He wouldn't try to stop the Security Officer since Captain Alex had put Geri in charge, but he didn't have to like the decision. "The least bad result was the subject was simply shot." He paused, obviously uncomfortable with the subject.

"And the worst?" Laurence's tone held an encouraging note for the Historian to continue.

"The worst?" Nigel paled. "The subject was frozen in the moment save for his heart which continued to beat. It exploded in his chest twenty four seconds into the experiment."

"....my god..." Laurence turned a look on Geri as if the Security Officer were carrying Satan himself on his shoulder.

Geri gave them both a flat look. "Ain't the same generation as those experiments. These were the newest. Nabbed 'em on my way out of Naviwerks." He smirked as he started towards the lift from the hold. They needed to get on the bridge. "Initial testing proved positive."

Laurence stared after Geri with his lips parted in shock. After a moment he closed his mouth and looked at Nigel who sighed with a shrug. When they started following the Security Officer he called out to Geri. "And what is to keep Agent Nash and his guard from having these rounds to use against us now?"

"Sabotaged the lot after I grabbed a few boxes." Geri stepped in the lift and turned an impatient look to Nigel and Laurence. "Won't stop them from making more. Couldn't get at the formulas. But they were back to manufacture and have to answer to government specs before they can be used. We don't. Now get in. We got a job to do."

"There." Geri pointed at the visual display where a light could be seen in the distance. He straightened from where he had been leaning on the back of Angel's chair to look out the windows, but with the naked eye the light was barely a speck. "Distance?"

Angel's fingers flickered over the controls on her console before she answered the Security Officer. "Just under a league." She looked up from the controls to the display, her lower lip caught between her teeth. "Could just be missionaries on their way to Rome, or traders. Need a closer look."

"Go silent, Miss Flynn." Captain Alex's voice came from the internal comm speakers. Dr. Hennessey wouldn't release her from medical, but she insisted on being kept informed. *"Veer off upon visual confirmation of identity."*

"Aye, Cap." Angel began flipping toggles on the console. "Running silent."

A moment later the constant low hum of the ship's power diminished until it disappeared all together. To the seasoned crew the sound was familiar and more like background noise. One grew used to it, and only noticed it when it was gone. However, none of them were comforted by its lack while the ship was in the sky. Angel now had the opportunity to put truth to her claim that the ship could coast.

Her shoulders were tight. Her brown hair pulled back into a ponytail did nothing to hide her tension as her fingers wrapped around the little used manual override wheel. Her expression was confident if focused as her eyes trained on the display. They had altitude enough to lose some height as she coasted the ship through the air, just as she had said it would. They lost speed without the boosting mini-thrusts from the engines, but that would work in their favor. Abrupt movement could attract the attention of any scouts and guards that might be further away from the camp.

Geri was still standing by the windows with his eyes on the distant light. When it grew bigger he came around the helm to better see the visual display. His brows furrowed as details around the campfire became more distinct. "Yep. That's them." Guards in yellow and blue striped uniforms could be seen walking near torches or cooking fires, and it became clear that this was a large encampment of about three hundred men. "Nash is there too."

"How can you tell?" Laurence had curiosity scrawled all over his face as he stepped forward.

Geri pointed at a tent in the middle of the encampment that was bigger than the rest. "Commander's tent. Regular guard wouldn't have it."

Identity confirmed, Angel turned the wheel and everyone stumbled a little as the ship turned sharply to starboard. "Gonna need to give her a boost soon, Cap or put her down."

"Understood, Miss Flynn." Alex's voice gave away how irritated she was to not be there on the bridge with them. The empty Captain's chair seemed larger somehow for only hearing her voice. *"Put her down then at your discretion. Mr. Reynolds, prepare to disembark."*

Geri thumped Angel's shoulder lightly with the side of his fist before he turned to head for the metal lattice work staircase out of the bridge. "Aye, Captain."

He jerked his chin at Nigel and Laurence in a beckoning gesture. "Let's go." He reached the landing to the outer hall by taking the short staircase in two strides, and disappeared from the bridge.

"Aye, Cap." Angel acknowledged her Captain before glancing quickly over her shoulder. "Good luck," she called to Nigel and Laurence then turned her entire focus back to flying the chrono-ship.

A few moments later the three men reached the lift, and were on their way to the hold. Geri noticed that Laurence kept staring at the rifle slung over his thick shoulder. The Security Officer frowned as he looked down at the smaller Horotech. "What."

"I thought you said we didn't have anything like what was used to shoot Captain de Sade on board." Laurence's voice was hesitant, but the Security Officer had to give him props for speaking up. Not that he would admit it out loud. The twerp still had to prove himself by Geri.

He smirked at Laurence and ignored the look of mild warning Nigel was trying to give him. "We don't." Geri made a show of hitching the rifle strap into a more comfortable position on his shoulder. "Nobody has anything like this. Built her special myself." His chuckle sounded like gravel being shaken together in his chest as he winked at Laurence.

"...ohgoodlord.." Laurence sighed as he pinched the bridge of his nose.

After the lift reached the hold Geri folded the gate to the side roughly then walked with confident strides towards the gangplank controls. He didn't look behind him to make sure that Nigel and Laurence were following. It was just assumed that they would fall in line. He could feel the ship losing speed and altitude through the vibrations from the hull beneath his feet. This landing wouldn't be the gentlest of touch downs. He grabbed a hold of some cargo netting that was dangling from the rafters, and wrapped it around his forearm. "You're gonna want to hold on to something."

Nigel directed Laurence to a girder to hold onto with a hand to the Horotech's back then found his own netting to cling to. Just in time too since Angel's voice came through the internal comms. *"I'm putting her down half a league from target behind a hill."*

Geri's jaw clenched but in anticipation instead of disapproval. This was his kind of mission. Captain Alex trusted him to get it done, and get her crew back safely. His hand tightened around the strap of the rifle. He wouldn't let her down.

"Brace yourselves. This could get a little bumpy."

That and the resounding thunk of the landing gear lowering into place was the only warning they had after that. Without being able to use the retro-ports to slow them down Angel would have to land the old fashioned way. There was an initial bump when the gear first touched the ground almost as if experimenting to see where it was, then a couple of lesser jarring before the ship was solidly on the ground. Rolling across the uneven ground created more disturbance than the actual landing had, but soon enough that was over as they jerked to a halt. All things considered the landing hadn't really been that bad. Public Transportation was worse.

As soon as the ship came to a stop Geri disentangled his arm from the cargo netting to go to the gangplank control. The protective brass cage was lifted and his hand hovered over the plunger as he looked up to the speaker. "Holding on all clear."

There was silence from the internal comms as Laurence and Nigel joined Geri. The Horotech had paled a bit while the Historian also seemed a bit edgy. He kept taking deep breaths every other inhale. Geri simply looked like he was preparing to go out for some milk.

Finally, Angel's voice came through. *"All clear. Not even a curious cow."*

That could either be good or bad in Geri's opinion. Best situation was that they were successful in landing covertly. At worst, they had been spotted by sentries, were expected and this was in fact a trap. But that was why he was well armed, and if their cover was blown then there was nothing to stop them from blasting off under full power. There had been no sign of another chrono-ship, but then they hadn't been able to engage the sonar without potentially giving themselves away. It was a risk, but if this worked it would be worth it. They take this swag, and their reputation would be settled on course. Geri understood Captain Alex's reasons for not giving up on the contract. He just didn't like the odds.

Like it or not, they were on a mission and his hand pushed hard on the plunger. There was a hiss that made him frown to hear as the hydraulics released the gangplank, lowering it to the ground gently. Geri pulled his pistol clear of the holster on his hip as he spoke quietly to Nigel and Laurence. "Keep to the plan. This ain't like Milan. Deviation will blow this to Hell. You ain't got a clear shot don't take it. Wait for the moment."

They weren't soldiers or guards. It was a fair bet that either of them would flinch when it came time. Nigel's hands didn't have a callous to speak of, and the closest Laurence had come to violence was harsh words. Geri would have preferred to do this alone, but that wasn't the Captain's orders. He had to trust them, but he'd keep an eye on them. "Let's go."

The three of them crept through the night. Laurence's feet seemed to find every branch and twig to step on which earned him increasingly sharp glares from Geri for every crack and snap. After a while, the Security Officer called them to a halt behind a stand of shrubs on the edge of a small forest. He said nothing until he was certain no one was near then spoke in a low whisper to Laurence and Nigel.

"Stay here," he growled out. "Keep quiet. If I'm not back in ten minutes get back to the boat."

Even in the darkness that seemed thicker without the lights of civilization, Laurence's eyes seemed rounder than normal, and he kept nervously pushing his spectacles farther up the bridge of his nose. "What do we do if someone other than you comes by?" His whisper held a shake to it that gave away his anxiety.

"Shoot 'em." Geri nodded to the pistol at the Horotech's hip. "Or hit 'em on the head with the nightstick." The nudge of his elbow to Laurence's arm just about knocked the smaller man over if not for Nigel being right next to him. "That's why you're armed, now stay put."

Geri could feel Laurence staring at him as he

crab walked to the side, staying low behind the bush until he could see around it. He drew his own pistol to hold at the ready with the barrel pointed up. When he didn't hear or see anything he was in motion, off into the trees.

For such a large man he could move silently when he wanted to. Naviwerks trained their security officers very well. At the time, Geri had thought that the special forces type of training he and his fellow guardsmen had received was a bit excessive, but if what they suspected was true, that Naviwerks had been preparing their own militia, then the training made sense. Regardless of the reason for the training, Geri was putting it to work now, and against the very people who had taught him.

Five minutes later he was about to turn back to gather up Nigel and Laurence when he found exactly what he had been hoping for. "Gotcha." He smirked to himself then quietly backed away. A few minutes after that he was back at the shrubs where he found that the Historian and the Horotech had actually done as he instructed. He also succeeded in startling the hell out of Laurence who fortunately only jumped instead of crying out.

"They've posted sentries not far ahead." Geri's expression was all business and grim as he looked at the other two men. "There's two of them. Looks to be about the right size for you two. Wellington and me will take 'em down hard and fast. Truss 'em up and hope the change of the guard ain't any time soon."

Nigel and Laurence exchanged a look as Geri replaced the pistol with a telescoping nightstick that got extended by a sharp flick of his wrist to the side. "Kane, you stay out of sight until I say otherwise. Nobody in Naviwerks knows you on sight so far as we know. Can't say the same for Wellington and me. The longer we keep it that way the better for us."

"Uh…right." Laurence looked honestly relieved that he wouldn't be involved in the impending violence, and nodded his head which made his spectacles slip down his nose again.

"C'mon." Geri hit Nigel in the arm with the back of his hand then began to creep down the line of the bushes as he had the first time. He heard the quiet sigh that came from the Historian, but could feel him come up behind him. After reorienting himself with where he had seen the sentries he snuck out from the bushes gesturing Nigel to follow.

Together they moved back the track that Geri originally took. In the back of his mind, Geri was surprised at how quickly and quietly Nigel was able to keep up with him. It wasn't something to be commented on now. Chances were Geri wouldn't bring it up later either, but he would keep the information stocked away in his mind for future use. The Security Officer just wasn't the sort to hand out compliments. He was quick to point out faults, however, and he made a mental note to have a talk with Laurence about stealth since he could hear the Horotech following them from several yards away.

He didn't take them back to exactly where he had seen the sentries. Instead, Geri circled them around to the side to get behind them. His intentions were to take out the two guards before Laurence caught up with them and gave them all away. His hand came to rest on Nigel's shoulder to get his attention then he pointed off to the right indicating that the Historian should take that sentry while Geri took the one to the left. Nigel nodded that he understood then moved off towards his mark with a grace that Geri hadn't noticed until he was in a position to be able to witness it. He only allowed it to distract him for a moment then he too was in motion to the left.

It was over quickly. Geri heard Nigel's target give a muffled grunt then hit the ground just before he swung his nightstick against the back of the head of his mark. He nudged the sentry with the toe of his boot after he had fallen, but the man was limp. Assured from that he went to check on Nigel's, but movement caught his attention. "Balls." He sneered then ran back the way they had come.

Laurence had indeed caught up with them, and had also attracted attention, but the guard was pointing what could only be a plasma pistol directly at Geri. The Horotech had taken the initiative to try to knock the sentry out from behind, but lacked the conviction for a solid strike of the nightstick. It was enough for the guard to flinch before he turned around to level the gun at Laurence. The movement was what had attracted Geri's attention. Before the trigger could be pulled however, Geri's nightstick rapped against his skull, dropping him to the ground just as limp as the other guards.

Geri was out of breath more from the shock of possibly having to report to Captain Alex that her Horotech had been killed, and he sneered at Laurence as his expansive chest heaved. His voice came out more as a low growl than anything human. "Next time swing like your mother's life is at risk. I might not be there to cover your ass." All Laurence could do was give a shaky nod as he gripped the nightstick with both hands and held it close to his chest. Having to be content with that, Geri swiped the back of his hand across his mouth then crouched to check out the guard he just dropped.

Nigel had approached and bent to pick up the plasma pistol that had fallen from the sentry's hand. "Hello. A rather un-fifteenth century weapon I'd say."

"Not exactly standard Papal Guard issue undergarments either." Geri turned a frown to the Historian as he pulled open the yellow and blue striped overcoat. Underneath it the sentry was wearing the black Kevlar lined security uniform with the scarlet Naviwerks logo over the right breast. "Looks like we were right." He spat to the side as he stood up. "Naviwerks is mucking around with history."

"So it would seem," said Nigel in the hushed tone they were keeping to. "But to what extent and why?"

"Figure it out later." Geri was pulling out length after length of monofilament cord from a sleeve built for it around the waistband of his pants. "We need to get these three secured and silent." He jerked his chin in Laurence's direction. "Start stripping 'em of their uniforms."

Laurence had stopped looking like a cornered rabbit, and more like the mouse he was as he swallowed then began working on the man who had pointed the gun at him. "Will this one fit you?" It was difficult to tell in the dark with the man prone on the ground.

Geri tilted his head as he looked at the unconscious sentry, sniffed then shrugged. "Well enough." He dropped the cording at Nigel's feet then turned to go haul over the other two sentries.

Between the three of them it didn't take too long to tie up the unconscious guards. By the time they were beginning to come around, they were tied to a tree and Geri had stuffed fabric knotted into balls in their mouths. The smirk he had on his face unsettled everyone but him as he patted the gunman's cheek. It earned him dark glares in return.

The uniforms were not a good fit even if Nigel did manage to pull off wearing the one he chose for himself. Laurence's was too long in the sleeves, and the pants gathered more around his calves rather than his knees. Geri's uniform didn't hang as loosely as intended, according to Nigel. The pants only came to above his knees and couldn't be fastened for as thick as his legs were. The Security Officer ended up slapping at Nigel's hands when the Historian dithered around too long with the cuffs of the pants. Nothing could be done about the uniforms here. Geri just hoped no one was paying too close attention when they got into camp.

Helms and halberds were found leaning against a tree nearby. The three picked one each. Geri chuckled under his breath when Laurence jammed a helm on his head and if fell forward over his eyes. "There is something wrong with you, Kane." With a halberd tucked against his elbow he yanked on the leather chin strap to Laurence's helm to tighten it. The helm still hid Laurence's eyes, but it wasn't falling in front of them anymore at least. That would have to do, and Geri grimaced a little before he turned to head off where they knew the camp was made. “Let’s get this over with.”

“Hang on.” Nigel had caught Geri by the arm. It earned him an irritated look. “If that is a whole camp of Naviwerks security how do you intend we get in and out again? As you said, you and I are both known by the company.”

Geri pulled his arm free as he turned to face Nigel. “They might recognize us sure, and most like are watching for us.” He let the halberd hang at a slight angle towards Laurence. “But they don’t know him.”

“Me?!” Laurence’s voice was a squeak.

Geri ignored him, and continued. “He takes point once we reach camp. Find us the first person near a tent, and shove them in. You and me slip under the wall and get the location of the model.” Before Nigel could ask the next obvious question he patted the holster with the hydrospray. “Then we bid him a goodnight.” He grinned. “We slip around for the best way in, take the swag and hail The William for a quick pick up.” At the disbelieving looks he was getting from Nigel and Laurence he sighed. “Are we or are we not pirates? If you have a better idea, I’m all ears.”

He watched the Historian and the Horotech look at each other. When they didn’t offer anything he snorted. “Then let’s go be pirates.” Once more he turned to walk off.

They managed to make it to the edges of the Papal Swiss Guard camp without further incident mostly due to the suggestions grumbled out to Laurence from Geri. The Horotech was nervous which made him twitchy in obvious ways, such as dropping the halberd more than once.

"Remember," growled Geri to Laurence. "Stick to the outer ring of tents. We'll be following from the shadows. Ain't no-one going to see us for the torchlight. Keep your head down, and repeat whatever greeting might be tossed your way." He gripped Laurence's shoulder as he gave the little man a nod. "Stick to that and you'll be fine."

"Yes, yes," came Laurence's nervous response. The nod he gave to Geri made his helm wobble on his head, but he just pushed it up as he swallowed. "Repeat what they say. Head down. First lone man near a tent. Got it." Then he stumbled a little, and almost lost the halberd again when Geri gave him a helpful push to get him going.

"Are you certain about this?" Nigel asked Geri in a hushed tone as they watched Laurence shuffle into the campsite.

"Nope." Geri's jaw tightened as Laurence looked to be having a moment of panic when two others dressed like the Guard walked by. They didn't so much as give him a second look or hesitate, but the Horotech hadn't started moving again. Before Geri could even think about finding a rock to chuck at that ridiculous helm Laurence made a decision to go to the right. "Don't have much choice by my reckoning. Tryin' to keep this as quick and quiet as possible. This is the best way." Without taking his eyes off of Laurence he put his hand to Nigel's shoulder and pushed to get him to keep pace with the Horotech.

Laurence passed a handful of opportunities Geri would have thought would suit their purposes. The

Security Officer was growing as edgy as the little man he had put all his hopes into, and was about to call it off entirely when finally Laurence stopped by a man sitting outside of a single person tent. When the Horotech engaged the man's attention Geri's entire body went tense. "Get ready," he whispered to Nigel.

The brief conversation seemed to have something to do with the strap of Laurence's helm. The man peered at it then nodded before he got up from the ground. As soon as he was briefly off balance, Laurence rammed full body into him, knocking him into the tent opening and followed him in.

Geri and Nigel made certain nobody was close enough to catch their movement then ducked under the back wall. The Security Officer never slowed down. It wasn't a large tent so he was able to grab the front of the Guard's overcoat in one fist while the other was raised to be slammed right into his face.

It never fell. The Guard had been ready to fight off one scrawny man, but had been entirely unprepared for the walking wall that was Geri. But it was what he said that kept the Security Officer from punching him. "Reynolds?"

Geri blinked as something about that voice resonated in his memory. His muscles unclenched, but he didn't lower his arm as he got a good look at the Guard's face. "…Fillion." Geri's fist finally lowered but he didn't let go of the man's uniform. His brows lowered in confusion as he stared.

Nigel came up next to Geri and looked at him quizzically. "You know this man?"

Geri nodded exactly once, but said nothing.

"Fool!" hissed the Guard they had succeeded in capturing. "What do you think you are doing? This is exactly what they want!"

"Shut up," Geri ordered as he gave Fillion a bit of a shake. He needed to think. For some reason he hadn't expected to run into someone any of them knew which was ridiculous since he and Nigel both had worked for Naviwerks for more than a handful of years. This complicated things.

Fillion looked from Geri to Nigel and frowned himself. Laurence was behind him watching the entrance with both hands wrapped tightly around the shaft of the halberd. "You can't be here, Reynolds. None of ya. Take your lot and just go while you can."

Geri's brain wasn't forthcoming with options on how to deal with the situation so he reverted back to the original plan and gave Fillion a shake again. "Where is it? Tell us where the model is and you'll live to see the next sunrise. I ain't kiddin' around, Fillion."

"It ain't here, ya idiot." Fillion wrapped his hand around Geri's wrist, but obviously wasn't trying to disengage him from the uniform.

Geri's frown grew deeper as he leaned towards their hostage. "What do you mean it ain't here?"

"This was all just a lure Nash drummed up to draw you out. And you went and fell for it." Fillion sighed as his eyes went to Nigel then back to Geri. "It's already in Rome snugged away in the vaults. Got there this mornin'. They were just waiting on your Captain to make her move."

Geri was growing angrier the more information Fillion gave them. "How'd they find out where we'd be?”

“Wait a moment,” Laurence came up finally, his voice barely heard. “How can we trust anything this man says? He could tell us anything Agent Nash wanted.”

Geri didn’t take his eyes off of Fillion, but there was nothing of mistrust there. And when he spoke it was quieter in inflection than tone. “Because he was my partner in the NSC.” At Laurence’s blank look Geri clarified. “Naviwerks Security Corp.”

“You think I fall for the loose helm strap every day, boy?” Fillion couldn’t turn with Geri having a grip on his uniform, but he did try to give Laurence a loose smirk.

No one was as big as Geri, but this man came close in girth if not height. Only slightly taller than Laurence, Fillion was square, older than all of them but solid. Geri knew if Fillion wanted to be free he could have broken his grip by now. That realization more than anything was what made Geri release him.

Fillion visibly relaxed then straightened his uniform. “You lot got to get out of here before someone higher up spots you. Forget the Gran Cavallo. It’s out of your reach now, and there’s more important things for you to chase.”

“What do you mean?” asked Nigel. His expression said that he was very curious about all of this. It made Geri scowl and cross his arms over his chest. They didn’t have the luxury to be poking around for answers, and Nigel had a tendency to ask touchy questions.

“I…can’t say too much.” For a moment it

looked as if Fillion was in pain, and he looked Geri in the eyes as he pressed his hand to the side of his head. "Can't, Reynolds. Not won't. So get that look off your face." A pleading look crossed his face briefly before it was hidden by years of military training, much like Geri. "They're…doing things. Injec-…" he broke off with a grunt of pain. His eyes shut tightly as he grit his teeth.

Geri reached out to put his hand on Fillion's shoulder. "Steady. Don't worry about it." He got it, and didn't like it one bit. Captain Alex wouldn't like it either. One more thing to deal with later.

A sad if grateful look appeared for a moment on Fillion's face before he hid that too. Geri's hand was brushed off his shoulder as his jaw tightened. "I can get you out of camp, but that's it."

"That's enough." Geri nodded as he took his hand back then turned for the back of the tent where he and Nigel had come in.

"Not that way," Fillion thumbed over his shoulder towards the actual entrance. "I know where all the posts are, and can thread you through." He waited until Geri had turned back around then Fillion aimed Laurence around with a hand to his shoulder, pushing him out the flap first, and following behind. "Good thing you mugged yourself some unifo-"

Fillion broke off as he kicked some dirt back at the two still in the tent then snapped to attention. Laurence was confused as he looked at Fillion who glanced at him out of the corner of his eye. He did a slight double take on Laurence then he snatched the spectacles right off the Horotech's nose. They were tossed behind them to the tent flap with a sharp snap of his hand.

"I say!" Laurence got kicked in the leg instantly.

"Shut up and stand at attention, boy or this is all going to Hell!" Fillion hissed that out sharply.

Nigel had fumbled with Laurence's spectacles while Geri peered through the tent flap. He saw Laurence suddenly snap to in place, but he couldn't see why. He had a sinking feeling he knew, and this could go really badly, really quick. A curse slipped out under his breath as as he slowly removed the rifle from his shoulder.

"What is it?" whispered Nigel just as confirmation of Geri's fears came into view trailing a quartet of personal guards behind him.

Geri crouched down inside the tent and lined up the sight. "Nash."

Fathom Out

IX
Too Close for Comfort

The circular view through the rifle scope panned up the backs of both Laurence Kane and Fillion. Geri Reynolds carefully positioned the rifle until Agent Nash came into view then centered the bastard in the crosshairs. There was a quiet click as he toggled the safety to the Off position then curled his finger around the trigger. This wasn't the ideal position, crouched in the tent behind Laurence and Fillion. Geri knew that very soon his line of sight would be obscured by Laurence's head as Nash approached, but it couldn't be helped. He was prepared to pop up and fire if need be. He didn't want to since that would blow their cover straight to Hell, but part of him was very tempted to put a hole in Nash's cranium. Captain Alex's reaction to that was what kept it as just an entertaining thought instead of a viable option.

"Do not move unless I do." Geri kept his tone of voice low and even as he gave Nigel Wellington the instruction. He could sense the Historian crouched behind and to the right of him.

"Yes, yes," came Nigel's clipped reply. "Of course."

The moment Geri dreaded came. Nash's approach put Laurence's head right between him and the rifle sight. Geri held his breath as his finger tightened on the trigger, ready to spring into action, but the Agent came back into sight without so much as a hesitation in his steps. The Security Officer's finger relaxed as he let out his breath. Now he was more interested in what Nash was saying as he passed by.

"…Wellington and Reynolds." Agent Nash's voice was a smooth baritone with hardly any inflection to it. Geri strained a little more to hear it. The Agent hadn't ever had much of a personality as far as he was concerned, but this was even more flat. "There has been no sign of Hennessey or Flynn, but I have no doubt they number amongst her crew. The other man I did not recognize. Make it a priority to learn his…" Nash's voice was lost then in the din of the camp as he and his group of guards moved away from the tent.

Geri stood up once he was certain Nash wasn't turning around. He slung the rifle over his shoulder with one smooth motion. Nigel had stood when he did, and the Security Officer could feel the Historian hovering behind him. Geri stared off in the direction Nash had gone from the slit of the tent flap while his mind worked over that whole encounter.

Outside the tent, Fillion grabbed Laurence's shoulder to haul the Horotech into the tent. Geri had backed up to let them in, but kept his eyes on the outside to make sure there were no other surprises. Laurence stumbled past him looking paler than normal.

"He didn't see me." Laurence's voice squeaked a little. "He looked right at me and didn't see me."

"Steady, man." Nigel placed his hand on Laurence's shoulder with a small smile on his face, and handed the Horotech his spectacles.

"You're welcome," said Fillion. He stepped to the back of the tent with his lips pressed into a thin line.

Laurence settled his spectacles on his nose and pulled the hooks behind his ears as he looked at Fillion. "Pardon?"

Fillion flicked a finger in the direction of Laurence's face as he nodded once. "No one wears gigs in the NSC, boy."

"They passed that then?" Geri left his position by the front of the tent to join them. The look he gave his ex-partner was incredulous to say the least. "There were rumors they were gonna push that through, but I didn't think they'd actually do it."

Fillion nodded as Nigel and Laurence stood there with looks of confusion on their faces. "Members of the prestigious Naviwerks Security Corp gotta have perfect, uncorrected vision in order to ensure an uninhibited performance." He tapped a finger next to the corner of his eye. "They start with lenses in your eyes, and put your name on a list for corrective surgery. I'm scheduled for next month."

Geri grimaced and spat to the side. "Bollocks."

"Makes no nevermind to me, but you gotta listen." Fillion grabbed onto Geri's arm with an intense expression hardening his face. "There's more in the company what are sympathetic than just me, and things you don't know." He flinched as if something pinched him in the side. "You get your arse to Rome. Forget the Gran Cavallo. That's a trap. Talk to Father Smythe. He's corporation and can point you towards what you really want."

"What is it we really want, Fillion?" Geri looked flustered. Captain Alex wouldn't take kindly to being told to abandon the contract, especially after being shot.

"Proof." The word was practically hissed out at them from Fillion just before he flinched again. It was more pronounced this time, and he took his hand back only to put it against the side of his head. "More… than just…greed." He grunted as the vein in his temple began to throb. "Things…people…should know…"

"Mr. Reynolds." Nigel touched Geri's arm and nodded towards Fillion. The man was obviously in serious pain for what seemed like no reason at all.

Geri pulled his arm away from Nigel, but nodded. "Enough, man. We'll figure out the rest on our own." Fillion had done more than right by them in Geri's opinion. It was time to leave, get back to the ship and talk to the Captain about going to Rome. But Fillion had other ideas since he grabbed Geri's arm once more in a more firm grip.

"Listen to me, damn it!" Geri's ex-partner was sneering with clenched teeth around the pain he was feeling as beads of sweat formed on his forehead. "Naviwerks is infiltrating key positions all through history. They don't care none about paradox no mo-…," he broke off with a grunt as a trickle of blood fell from one nostril, but he pressed on. "Find out…why…then tell the…world."

"All right!" growled Geri as he plucked Fillion's hand from his arm. He kept hold of his wrist in a tight grip to startle his former partner out of his stubbornness. "We'll go. My word on it." He ignored the looks that Nigel and Laurence gave him for promising something without checking with Captain Alex first. He was more concerned about whatever was causing Fillion's nose to bleed. He watched the man swipe his sleeve under his nose then released his wrist when no more blood appeared on his face.

Fillion lifted his freed hand as he nodded, still dabbing at his nose with his sleeve. "Don't keep the Swiss Guard uniforms or you'll stand out. Wear monks' robes or something. When you get into the Vatican ask for Father Smythe. Grab your swag then get out. Naviwerks ain't as present here as other times, but they ain't absent neither." He smoothed his hand over his uniform, leaving a red smudge on part of the yellow fabric. "Now let's get you outta here."

Fillion moved to the back of the tent where another flap was tied down. He began working the knots loose as Geri grabbed Laurence by the shoulder and pushed him in front of him and Nigel. He wanted the Horotech where he could keep an eye on him this time. "We trussed up some guards in the woods to get these uniforms. Someone's gonna miss them soon. Could be trouble that comes back to you," Geri said to Fillion's back.

Fillion just snorted in wry amusement. "Won't be my problem no more since I ain't coming back here."

Nigel gave Geri a confused look before he asked

quietly, "What do you mean, Sir?" There was wariness in his voice that Geri understood, but he could have told the Historian that his train of thought was way off course. He was proven correct a moment later.

"Relax, son." Fillion smirked over his shoulder as he got the last knot loose then held open the flap. "I ain't looking to go pirate and join your band of merry men. I aim to wander off and blend in with the surroundings." He put his hand on Laurence's arm to get him moving through the tent flap and out the back. "Maybe find me a plump fifteenth century Italian woman and settle down." He waggled his brows with a chuckle as Geri rolled his eyes.

"But," Nigel stopped in front of Fillion as he followed Laurence. "You will be stranding yourself here. Aren't there people who will miss you at home?"

Fillion gave the Historian a hard edged but kind smile. "I said my goodbyes a long time ago, son. Besides, I can think of worse ways to live out the end of my days." He patted Nigel on the arm then gave him a push towards the tent flap. "Now go."

The smile Nigel gave Fillion was a little sad, but he nodded before he ducked out of the tent. It was Geri's turn to stop by Fillion then, and the two men exchanged a moment of silence. It was broken by Fillion's fist connecting with Geri's shoulder. Surprise widened Geri's eyes as his hand covered the spot Fillion had just punched. It hadn't been hard enough to hurt, but he rubbed his shoulder all the same.

Fillion pointed up at Geri as he arched a brow. "Don't start. I'll be all right. Just get." He jerked his head in the direction of the tent flap.

Geri actually smiled as he nodded. He was glad that he had to duck his head so much to get through the flap; it would keep Nigel and Laurence from seeing his expression. He had fond memories of being teamed up with Fillion. They hadn't worked together for years, but now that Geri knew Fillion was stranding himself in the past, he knew he would miss the man all the more. He just didn't want the other two to know that. Nigel would never let him live it down. Cheeky bastard of an Historian.

*****

Captain Alexandria de Sade was resting on the examination table of the medical bay. Her side hurt where the plasma round had gone through, but it was the familiar tingling ache of the fast track meds she had been given doing their job. If she took it easy, the stitches could come out in a couple of days. In a week she would be left with nothing more than a fresh scar. *If* she took it easy, that is. Alex was not the type to lie about and do nothing. She had a ship to run, a reputation to create and a crew to take care of, but for Dr. Hennessey's sake she was lying there with her eyes closed, and as relaxed as she was liable to be.

"You are not fooling me, young lady," Dr. Hennessey said as he organized a drawer of instruments. He didn't bother to turn around.

Alex couldn't help but smile, but she kept her eyes closed. "I never thought I was."

The speaker in the upper corner of the medical bay crackled giving them a brief warning that Angel was about to hail them. *"Landside team returning empty handed, Cap. Again."*

Alex had opened her eyes as soon as her Pilot Angel Flynn had started talking. She turned a frown on Dr. Hennessey after hearing Angel's report. "Have them report to the mess hall, Miss Flynn." Then she began to sit up with every intention of getting to her feet. "And get us airborne as soon as they are on board."

"Aye, Cap." The speaker crackled again as Angel shut off the internal comm.

Alex swung her legs over the edge of the exam table, but she hesitated for a moment before trying to put weight on her feet. Dr. Hennessey had turned around to skewer her with a disapproving look as he crossed his arms. "You think that your body has no limitations, but it does, Alexandria."

"I have to meet them, Abraham." Alex's voice was tight, but there was an edge of pleading to it only someone who had known her as long as the Doctor had would detect. "Something went wrong." *Again* was the word she left off. "This contract is going south. I need to be up and making decisions or the whole plan is dead in the birthing."

Dr. Hennessey's mutton chop whiskers bristled as he grumbled under his breath then he huffed out a sharp breath as he tromped over to a narrow closet. He reached inside after pulling open the door. "If you are going to insist on this course of madness," he turned around to hold a cane towards Captain Alex, "then at least use this." He let out with a harrumph. "If only to make an old man happy."

It wouldn't do to be openly amused by the Doctor so Alex kept her lips tightly together before she took the cane from him. "Very well."

It was a lovely cane made of heat-hardened mahogany that was polished smooth, then coated in resin to make it shine. As Captain Alex ran her fingers over the surface, the bulbous ivory head of the cane caught her attention. A skull without a jawbone was carved in relief with a pair of femurs crisscrossing behind it. Underneath was a ribbon upon which was engraved the words *Captain Alexandria* in a scrolling script. It was so over the top pirate that Alex sighed as she lifted the cane in Dr. Hennessey's direction. "Cute." She didn't know what was worse: that he felt the need to give her some pirate flair or the fact that he had the cane made under the assumption that she would need it.

"Come on, Doctor." Alex let the cane swing down until the tip connected with the tile floor with a quiet clack. It proved to be the perfect height for her, which was a little surprising considering how short she was. She assumed the good Doctor had it adjusted or made to order. She let the cane take her weight as she took an experimental step and found that it did indeed help reduce the stress on her injury. Not that she would admit that out loud. "Let us find out what went wrong this time."

She and Dr. Hennessey could feel the gangplank for the hold activate as they left the medical bay. The vibrations could be felt through the hull especially without the engines running. That changed when Angel turned them on in preparation for take off. They had come in running dark and silent, but Captain Alex wasn't quite as worried about discretion now. If the campsite hadn't belonged to Nash her crew would have been back long before this. Let him see how close she had been.

Navigating the stairs was a practice in hiding her pain. Alex clenched her teeth together every time she had to lift her leg. Not that she was putting much weight on it, but lifting it from one step to the next pulled on muscles that were not happy in the slightest. She knew Dr. Hennessey was watching her every move. She also knew she was not concealing her discomfort from him very well, but if he wasn't going to say anything she wasn't going to stop.

By the time the three men arrived in the mess hall, Angel had the ship in the air, and Captain Alex was settled in her chair at the head of the dining table. She had managed to school her expression to a cool neutral, but instead of hiding the cane as if she were embarrassed by it she had it next to her chair with her hand resting on the skull. Her eyes picked over their expressions in an attempt to get an idea of what mood she should be in: Nigel looked worried, and Laurence looked pale and a bit shaken, but that seemed to be normal for her Horotech. But it was her Security Officer that would be the most telling. Geri's eyes landed on the cane, and Alex arched a brow as if daring him to react in any way to its presence. He just looked uncomfortable yet determined.

"Well?" Her voice broke the silence, causing Laurence to startle. Captain Alex was annoyed by the delays. That much was obvious by her tone. This contract was going nothing like she had planned. It should have been a simple retrieval to establish the reputation of the crew.

Unsurprisingly Geri stepped forward to the

opposite end of the table to give the report. "The model was never in the campsite. Gathered intelligence said it made it to Rome this morning. The site was a trap laid by Agent Nash."

"Gathered how?" It wasn't that Captain Alex doubted the validity of Geri's information, but instinct told her to ask for clarification.

"By an informant." Geri's expression grew tight, as did his tone of voice. Captain Alex turned her head just a little to the side as she took note of that small change. Not a lot affected Geri like this so she was glad that she followed her instinct.

"Can we trust them?" she asked even though she already knew the answer. Geri would have mentioned the questionable nature of the information if he wasn't certain of it.

True to her expectations he nodded. "We were met by a man I was partnered with in the NSC. Name of Fillion. He stuck his neck out to keep Kane from getting pinched by Nash." Geri jerked his head towards Laurence who looked abashed as he cleared his throat quietly.

"And did we make good on that debt?" Captain Alex turned an assessing glance to Laurence, but Geri pulled her attention back

"Didn't need to." Geri pushed forward when Captain Alex looked irritated by that. "He was lookin' for us. Said the Gran Cavallo was bait to lure us out." He hesitated when Captain Alex's eyes narrowed. "But he said we got to go to Rome anyway. Said there's information there we got to have in our possession. Stuff to use against Naviwerks."

Alex's fingers had begun to drum as her expression grew thoughtful. "I am beginning to believe that this contract was a set up." The why was obvious, but how Naviwerks managed it was what stumped her. She had been the one to approach the contact in the Sforza Museum. It occurred to her, however, that she had come up with the idea after having seen the model on a list of possible artifacts to retrieve before she had left Naviwerks. It was quite possible that the company had already been in contact with the museum before her, and they made a deal with the corporation. In the end Captain Alex didn't believe it really mattered how it came about. The Gran Cavallo was a lure, and she refused to chase it any further.

"I am inclined to agree with you, Captain." Nigel had been quiet during Geri's explanation. He spoke up now with a gravity that wasn't typical from him; there wasn't a trace of his usual smug amusement. He had even addressed her by rank instead of calling her some pet name designed to annoy her. It was enough to get Captain Alex's complete attention.

"The corporation has been one step ahead of us this entire time, and I for one am tired of being led by my nose." Nigel sniffed indignantly as if his nose comment was more than a metaphor.

"Agreed." There came a time when one stopped chasing the rabbit and chose a different game. Alex was no fool to keep clawing at a snipe hunt. She wasn't pleased by any stretch of the imagination, but that just fueled her determination to defeat Naviwerks and their agenda.

She turned her attention back to her Security

Officer, her pale blue eyes sharp with her displeasure. "Mr. Reynolds, I would like to hear more about this information we should collect from Rome."

Geri cleared his throat once more as he nodded. He placed his hands behind his back as though standing at attention before he began to speak. "According to Fillion, Naviwerks is doin' far more than just stockpiling artifacts and chargin' their customers inflated prices. He said there's proof of what they're doin' in Rome that we and the world need to know. Something about infiltrating key points in history. He said to contact Father Smythe, who would point us in the right direction."

Alex's brows lifted. She recognized the priest's name from her time in Naviwerks as they had served together on a ship when Alex had been a Second Mate. He had proven himself more loyal to the crew than company. Whoever this Fillion was, mentioning Smythe vetted his reputation in her mind. "I thought he had left the company."

"Looks like he's been planted here as a priest along with some of the Corps as members of the Swiss Guard." Geri gave Captain Alex a knowing look that made her frown even more.

"Yes, I am beginning to get a better picture," she said through clenched teeth. The rhythmic drumming her fingers had been doing against the ivory skull picked up speed since she couldn't get up and pace.

Nigel stepped up next to Geri then, and placed his hand on the large man's shoulder as he spoke to Captain Alex. "It is worse than you might imagine. The man who assisted us, this Fillion, something was causing him pain that we could not see." Geri gave him a sharp look as he tugged his shoulder out from under Nigel's hand, but the Historian ignored it all. "It seemed to me as if every time he attempted to speak on a controversial subject he felt pain. Indeed, at one point the man gave himself a nose bleed."

Whatever reaction her crew might have expected from her was not what they got. Captain Alex suddenly looked to Dr. Hennessey where he stood leaning against a kitchen counter. They seemed to hold a silent conversation that ended in the Doctor giving a resigned sigh. He shook his head while Captain Alex looked troubled.

Laurence, who had maintained his silence the whole time, looked at each member of the crew before his gaze settled on the Captain. "You know something about this. Don't you." He looked over at the Doctor. "Or at least suspect." His tone was not as accusatory as his words.

"We saw documents," said Dr. Hennessey in a subdued voice. "Schematics and test results." Captain Alex's fingers tightened around the cane head as the Doctor spoke. Her eyes gained a haunted look as she stared at the surface of the dining table. "*Behavior Modification* they called it. It utilizes the introduction of nano-technology into the nervous system. The nanites attach themselves to strategic control centers. The programming is done by the same software engineers that designed the tracking and control systems of the chrono-ships. If the program is running then yes, the man's pain centers would have been activated by the nanites as a warning." He gestured helplessly with one hand then let it fall limp at his side.

“We?” Geri’s tone was clipped and angry. When the Captain lifted her eyes, she was surprised by his glare.

“Yes,” she answered quietly. There was regret in her eyes, but she kept her expression stern and would not look away from her Security Officer. “I had found the documents, been told some of the details during my promotion meeting. I took them to Dr. Hennessey when I left the company.” That was as much as she was willing to explain to anyone in her crew, and there was plenty that she was leaving out. There had been a very good reason why she had left without saying a word to Nash that had nothing to do with assuming he would not turn against Naviwerks. But it was nobody’s business why she had lied to them about actually having the documents during her departure speech before they arrived in Milan.

Geri looked ready to spit nails, as the absent Angel would put it, even more than usual. The muscles in his jaw worked as he clenched and unclenched his teeth. Captain Alex refused to look away from him, but she did note that Laurence backed away from the Security Officer. Even Nigel who was normally not the type to melt into the background took a step to the side.

“You never thought to share this information with the rest of the crew?” Geri’s voice was practically a growl. “Captain. We still have friends in the company.”

Alex almost came up out of her chair with her lips curled into a sneer of contempt, but Dr. Hennessey quickly stepped forward. He motioned for her to remain seated then pointed at the Security Officer. “Belay that, Mr. Reynolds." He turned a sharp look on Geri. "She made mention of this very fact before we left. The documents were not dated. She had no reason to believe that they were implementing the procedures, let alone on the rank and file. Everything in those documents suggested only Agents Tier 2 or higher were slotted for modification. Possibly Tier 3."

Silence descended upon the mess hall after that with all eyes going to Captain Alex. They all knew what Tier Nash was, and that he had at least been her partner for some time. Alex could have cheerfully jabbed Dr. Hennessey in the gullet with the cane for letting that bit of information fall out.

Dawning realization replaced the confusion on Laurence's face as his mind pieced it all together. Captain Alex almost envied him the lack of experience that taught one to guard their expressions. She was far too good at it even if she was grateful for the ability at this moment. Agent Nash was not her favorite subject. What may or may not have been done to him by Naviwerks with or without his permission was a thought she had been avoiding. She certainly wasn't going to open it to the floor for discussion.

She locked eyes with her Security Officer. A silent battle of wills began between them. Geri was angry that she had withheld information. Alex was firmly of the opinion that she was Captain of this ship, and her decisions were final. But Geri knew what Nash had been to her. He hadn't liked it, but it hadn't been his call. What made him finally lower his eyes first wasn't his unshakable loyalty to his Captain, but his comprehension of how much she must be hiding behind those cold blue eyes. He wouldn't add to it.

When she saw Geri accept her authority she gave the slightest of nods. "We will go to Rome." She sounded calm and in control, but there was a note of stress to her voice. "Miss Flynn has detected no other ships in the area so we will beat Nash there. We will touch down to let Mr. Reynolds and Mr. Kane off to meet with Father Smythe, and retrieve the information we require. Miss Flynn will keep *The William* in the upper strato where we will wait for word." Nigel opened his mouth, but Alex gave him a look that clearly said she would brook no argument about her orders. When he sighed quietly with a nod she returned to looking at her crew. "Get to work."

Geri gave her a tight nod before he turned to leave. He caught hold of Laurence's shoulder to pull him along with him. Captain Alex wasn't making a move to get up out of her chair. Dr. Hennessey looked at her for a moment, but saw something in her expression that made him decide to leave her alone. He too made to leave the mess hall but not without placing a hand on her shoulder on his way past.

That left Nigel. He hadn't moved a muscle. Alex looked at him and arched a brow. He gave her a mild chastising look in return then walked down the table towards her. "I am so sorry, sweetie."

Captain Alex's fingers tightened enough around the cane top that her knuckles turned white. "For what?" It was just barely a question.

"Nash," replied Nigel not ungently. He stopped when he got to the end of the table, and sat down regardless of the frown she gave him. "This cannot be easy for you."

Alex's frown deepened as she turned her face away. "Leave it alone."

Nigel reached out to place his hand over hers where it rested on the cane. "Sweetie, you are possibly one of the strongest persons I have ever met, but you are still a person. Nobody would blame you for-"

"I said leave it alone, Lord Wellington." It wasn't often that Alex raised her voice, but she did so now as she cut off whatever Nigel was going to say. Her head had snapped back around. The look she gave him was filled with anger, but there was a shine to her eyes that she couldn't hide.

Nigel pulled back as if she had actually struck him. He wasn't just surprised, he was hurt, and he slowly took his hand back. "Yes. Yes, of course, Captain." He lowered his eyes from her as he stood up, and turned to go.

Captain Alex felt like something that might ooze up from under the landing gear, and reached out to catch Nigel's hand. The Historian was faster than that. She missed as he laced his fingers together at his waist. "Nigel, wait. Forgive me."

He glanced back over his shoulder, and drummed up a ghost of a smile. "Nothing to forgive, my dear."

But Alex could tell by his tone of voice that Nigel was stung. She watched him quietly leave the mess hall. Once she was alone she let out a sigh and rubbed at her forehead with her fingers.

X
Holy See, Rome

Angel had *The William's Hunt* touch down outside of Rome while it was still dark to allow Geri and Laurence to disembark. Following Captain Alex's orders, the Pilot lifted off immediately afterward to put the ship into a holding pattern in the upper stratosphere while the two men went on their way towards the Holy See. Fifteenth century monks' robes and cowls were easier to put on than the uniform of the Papal Swiss Guard, and Laurence was relieved to be more comfortable than he had been during the caper thus far, at least physically.

The tension from the mess hall seemed to linger however. Laurence was hesitant to break the silence that existed between himself and the Security Officer, but there came a point when it was just too much to take. Laurence looked up at Geri where he could see part of the Security Officer's grim profile unobscured by the cowl. "Are you truly angry with Captain de Sade?" He tensed in anticipation of a telling off at the very least.

He watched Geri's lips tighten into a thin line. The Security Officer didn't answer right away, but seemed to think about the matter first. Laurence was learning that for as much of an ape as Geri appeared to be at first, there was a strong mind in that thick skull and the man made good use of it more often than not.

Finally, Geri's gravel like voice broke the silence. "Yes and no," was his surprising answer. Laurence hadn't expected such honesty since Geri didn't like him. "We all still have friends in Naviwerks. If there was a chance they were being tampered with we had a right to know."

Geri never took his eyes from the road before them, yet somehow Laurence felt more included in this conversation than in any previous exchange. "But it's her ship. I get why she kept it quiet. Would have compromised our convictions if we had any sort of sympathy for those still workin' for the company."

"But the information would have come to light sooner or later, don't you think?" Laurence asked. He felt a bit bolder since Geri was actually talking to him instead of at him.

The Security Officer nodded before he turned a hard look to the Horotech. "All kinds of information's gonna come out of this, and ain't none of it designed to put smiles on our faces. The Captain's tryin' to stay one step ahead of it all for our sake, not hers. So you mind me, boy. Don't you for one minute think she slighted us. Might not agree with the how of her way of decision making, but I ain't never gonna argue the why." He turned his attention back to the road. "Like it or not that includes her takin' you on."

Laurence blinked as he stared at Geri's profile for a moment, his lips parted in stunned silence. That might have been the most insight into the man that Geri had allowed Laurence to have. It gave the Horotech hope. "I see." He couldn't help the slight smile that curled his lips, but he could face forward so that the Security Officer couldn't see it. "Thank you."

They made their approach from the northwest in order to avoid walking through all of Rome to get to St. Peter's. Laurence was doing his best not to gape like a tourist, but it was difficult at times. This was his first trip back in time, and while he wasn't Catholic, seeing the Sistine Chapel not long after it had been completed was humbling. Geri had to clear his throat at him a number of times to keep him focused on the job at hand. The glower on the Security Officer's face was met with a sheepish smile from Laurence, and the Horotech redoubled his effort to keep his attention where it belonged.

When they reached the courtyard Geri's hand landed on Laurence's shoulder. "Probably a safe bet everyone here talks Latin or Italian or somethin' which means you do the talking until we get to Father Smythe."

Laurence nodded, but his eyes were looking past Geri. His face was paler than normal again which made Geri glance over his shoulder. A couple of men in the Swiss Guard uniform were walking by about ten yards away from them. Geri looked back to Laurence as he gave the Horotech's shoulder a squeeze. "Ignore 'em. We belong here, remember?"

"Right," said Laurence as he nodded beneath

the cowl. "We belong here. On mission or quest or… something."

"Pilgrimage," said Geri with failing patience.

"Pilgrimage." Laurence smiled in gratitude. "Right. Got it."

Geri sighed as he turned Laurence by his shoulders then started walking again. "C'mon. Let's find a choir boy."

"But if we are on pilgrimage then wouldn't it stand to reason that we might very well speak-.." Laurence began, but Geri interrupted him with a growl.

"Don't get creative." The Security Officer's hand tightened on Laurence's shoulder until the Horotech gave a small cry of protest and cringed. "Just do the talking."

It didn't take them long to find a young boy in servant's livery who was jogging by with a bucket in his hand. Laurence hailed him and politely asked where they could find Father Smythe. The boy pointed towards the library buildings as he told them to ask for the priest there. He didn't wait to see if they had any other questions, just scampered off to complete whatever errand he was on, which left Laurence and Geri no choice but to continue on to the library.

They repeated the routine with another servant after they entered the first library building. Upon inquiring about Father Smythe, they were asked to remain in the vestibule while the servant left to locate the priest.

"Fillion was right," mumbled Geri as his eyes took in the details of everyone within sight. Laurence could only assume he was attempting to discern who was or was not a plant of Naviwerks.

"About what?" Laurence looked up at the Security Officer in curiosity.

"It's easier to move around here, and not." Geri turned his attention solidly onto Laurence. "Been off ship in a number of times, and so long as you didn't draw attention to yourself you'd be in and out without trouble. But here," his eyes flickered around them, "something's hangin' in the air. Like bein' watched."

"Well," offered Laurence. "It *is* the church of all churches." He turned to watch a couple of men that seemed to be in deep discussion as they walked by. Something to do with God and the rising of the sun. "There is bound to be a sense of the omniscient, I should think."

"The what?" Geri looked at Laurence as if the Horotech had just spoken in some alien language.

"The all knowing," Laurence supplied with a patient smile.

Geri frowned as he looked around them again. "Let's just hope Naviwerks ain't reachin' to make themselves into a deity then." He let out a long sigh. "Where did he have to go to find this guy? Back to Milan?"

Laurence too was growing impatient, but with more wariness than anything. "I would assume that the good Father might have been put off from the code word the Captain gave us."

Geri smirked at the smaller man. "You're Brother Sadie, by the way."

Laurence let out with a long-suffering sigh as he pinched the bridge of his nose. "Yes, I am well aware of that."

Fortunately for Laurence the servant returned

and gave them both a nod before he spoke quietly in Italian. *"Father Smythe asks that you meet him in the library garden. Follow me."*

Laurence looked to Geri then turned to follow the servant. The Security Officer didn't bother to ask for a translation. He just fell into step beside the Horotech.

The servant led the two men through an archway into a small garden courtyard in the middle of the library buildings. Stone benches were placed strategically beneath olive trees or in the sun next to fountains. Some were occupied by men either in prayer, reading a scroll or book, or in quiet conversation. He led them towards a solitary man who looked to be in inner contemplation on one of the benches beneath a couple of shade trees. The servant stopped some distance away then gestured towards the man as he gave Laurence and Geri another bow-like nod. As the two kept walking towards the man on the bench, the servant left to return to his duties.

"I admit that I expected the woman herself when I was told to meet with Sadie." The man's voice was quiet, gentle even. When he lifted his head, he was revealed to have a thin and slightly drawn face. Long years of worry and care etched lines on a face not old enough to bear them. Light green eyes seemed haunted but their gaze was steady on the two men standing before him. The smile he gave them was edged with sadness.

"You're Smythe?" asked Geri. Laurence was more than happy to let him take over from here.

"I am, yes," answered the man in priest's robes. "And you would be members of her crew. I am glad that you found me."

"Fillion gave us your name. Pointed us in your direction and said you had information for us." Geri's voice was even and neutral of inflection.

Father Smythe nodded slowly, his eyes lowering to look at the space between them. "Good. The net is working then."

"Net?" Laurence asked.

Father Smythe nodded again. "There are many of us in Naviwerks who dislike what the company is doing, but we have been unable to do anything, feeling as if the machine is larger than the parts." He lifted his eyes once more to Geri and Laurence, and there was a cunning spark in them. "Until Captain de Sade made her move. Now we have rallied together to support her. We have sworn to help when and where we can."

Geri and Laurence looked at each other for a moment in bewilderment before the Security Officer turned a questioning look back to Smythe. "Does she know about this?"

The priest shook his head. "Not that I am aware of. We have only just begun. Some have messages to give her. Some, like myself, have information."

"But won't you get caught?" asked Laurence with more than a little concern in his voice. It was a terrible risk these people were taking upon themselves, but Father Smythe just shrugged as if the idea was negligible.

"We expect it to happen from time to time, but consider the cost worth the results if it means the corporation will be exposed." The priest ran a hand over his thinning hair. "And nobody knows how many of us there are or the identities of everyone involved so there will always be some left to rebuild if many of us are caught."

Geri gave a quiet snort, but Laurence could tell by the smirk on the Security Officer's face that he was impressed. "A network of spies."

Father Smythe nodded again and smiled. "Just so." Then he gave a quiet chuckle. "She wasn't the first one to defy the corporation. Just the first to steal a ship." His smile faded once more as if it were too weak to be maintained for long. "She needs to know. The company is…doing things. Experimenting on their own." He shook his head as he clasped his hands together in his lap. "I have no proof of it beyond my own experience with a fellow I used to research with in the libraries."

That piece of information let Laurence and Geri know that Smythe was a Historian for Naviwerks. It made sense that he was posing as a priest and worked in the libraries here in Rome.

Geri nodded to him with a look of disapproval on his face. "We know. The Captain has a lead on it."

Smythe's hands parted as he shook his head, his eyes on his empty and ink stained palms. "One day he was the man I had to my house for dinner. The next he seemed…dead inside." He turned a sad look up to them.

Laurence felt his heart go out to the man. The Horotech didn't have friends to speak of, but he could not help but wonder what it must be like to have someone you know change so drastically overnight. It made for a very lonely and helpless feeling even vicariously.

"It's on the list." Geri placed his hand on Father

Smythe's shoulder with an intense expression turned down to the man. Laurence was learning this much about the Security Officer very quickly: he was a man of his word, and he did not give it lightly.

Father Smythe gave Geri a tired, but grateful smile as he patted the hand on his shoulder. "Thank you." He took in a deep breath then lifted his smile some more. It looked forced. "I don't want to waste your time any further so I will get right to the point." He looked to Geri not Laurence, but the Horotech couldn't blame him. The large man was obviously the one in charge.

"Naviwerks has been placing trusted or controlled members of the Corps in key points in history. Some of us that knew this was happening thought it was simply so that they would have an anchor, or someone who could be considered a local for more ease of movement anachronistically. What we discovered was far from what we assumed."

Laurence glanced at Geri and grew anxious about what they would be told next. He was afraid he knew what was coming, and sent up a prayer that he was wrong.

"They are altering history." Father Smythe's words confirmed Laurence's fears. The Horotech removed his spectacles to rub at his eyes as Geri made a sound not unlike a growl.

"Are you certain?" asked a very angry Geri. "How could we know for sure? Everything would change around us. Records. History books. Even those stupid vid shows."

"Horotechnology 101," said Laurence in a quiet

voice. "Tampering with time is immoral in that it alters the memories of the entire planet without choice. The dangers inherent in such a venture outweigh any benefit that might be wrought."

Father Smythe turned a grim smile to Laurence. "Who do you think wrote the handbook?"

Laurence gaped at the priest for a moment with his spectacles still in his hand as his mind processed what Smythe just told them. It was…frankly atrocious! It went against everything he had been taught at university when it came to ethics. But of course it made sense that Naviwerks designed and wrote the curriculum since they were the only employment available to Horotechs. With a sad sigh escaping him, he replaced his spectacles onto his nose.

"There's proof, ain't there?" Geri had taken his hand back and crossed his arms over his chest. "That's what Fillion was talking about."

This time when Father Smythe smiled there was more confidence in it. He nodded exactly once. "There is proof." He stood up from the bench and walked between the two men towards and archway leading back into one of the library buildings. "Come with me."

Laurence and Geri followed Father Smythe in silence, both of them lost in their thoughts over this new information. For Laurence, this upset everything he had been taught to believe in as a chrono-scientist. One didn't overturn the course of historical events! Just because they could go back in time, didn't give them the right to change what happened. One did not play God. These were values that he and the rest of his fellow Horology students had instilled in them since the very first day of university. And yet obviously, there were Horotechs deeply involved in Naviwerks that were betraying those values. Laurence already didn't understand humanity because of how people treated each other; now he was further saddened for the human race.

Father Smythe led them through arched hallways that were in desperate need of repair. In fact, the entire wing of the library seemed to be cracked or crumbling in places. Dust was a constant fog of varying density while small piles of plaster and stone formed in corners. Laurence spied at least two people with bins and brooms cleaning up what rubble crumbled from the wall or ceiling. It was somewhat strange to see such disrepair at this point in history; it was easy to forget that not every building constructed in these times was as long lasting as the Sistine Chapel on the first try.

Father Smythe glanced back and noticed Laurence's reaction to the condition of the library. He smiled a little as he slowed to walk beside the Horotech. "This library has been around a long time already. Soon they will begin to repair and rebuild. It's one reason why I specifically requested that I be assigned to this time so that I could witness the reconstruction as it happens."

Laurence turned a surprised look to the priest. "You requested…" Then his quick mind worked it out. What better way for the Historians to know their trade in connection with traveling through time than to actually live in the past? Naviwerks truly was both impressive and frightening. He gave Father Smythe a smile and nodded. "I see."

The three men stopped by the archway of a

side room. Inside could be seen a few priests at study or writing notations at desks of varying sizes. Father Smythe leaned closer to Geri and Laurence, his voice barely a whisper. “There is a restricted section to the left of the main shelves near the back that contains records of events Naviwerks has altered or has plans to. You will not be able to mistake it since it is enclosed in a metal cage, and guarded.” Geri frowned as he peered over Laurence’s head into the room, but looked back quickly enough when Father Smythe put his hand on the Security Officer’s arm. “Don’t worry about them. I will create a distraction outside the windows that will draw them out of the room. Just keep busy, maintain a low profile, and wait for my signal.” He patted the arms of both men, and gave them a curt nod. “Good luck, gentlemen, and give my best to your Captain.”

He pushed between Laurence and Geri, and was a few paces away before Laurence called out to him in a hushed tone. “Excuse me, but,” he paused with an uncertain, but quizzical expression, “why Sadie?”

A secretive smile formed on Father Smythe’s face after he heard the question. “Everybody calls her Alex. I told her she was far too womanly for that. So I,” his eyes looked skywards as he thought for a moment, “softened her last name.”

Geri gave a quiet snort, but Laurence saw that he was trying to contain a smirk. Laurence didn’t bother to try. He let Father Smythe see the smile that came to his face. “Ah. Thank you, Father.” He and the priest exchanged a nod then Father Smythe turned to hurry off.

After the priest disappeared from view, Geri and Laurence went into the wing. Geri grabbed the first thick book he saw then led Laurence to a tall book stand. With hardly any respect for the tome, the Security Officer opened the book to a random page and set it on the stand. He pulled Laurence in close so it would appear as if the two of them were discussing the contents.

"Don't look around," said Geri in a quiet growl. "There are two Naviwerks Papal Guards by the gate to the restricted se-"

"My God!" The only thing that kept Laurence from getting slapped was that he kept his exclamation quiet. His eyes were glued to the book Geri had set on the stand so unceremoniously. "This is a copy of the Vulgate."

"I don't care if it's a flip book of your grandma's knickers." Geri hunched in order to snarl that at Laurence who didn't seem to hear him.

The Horotech chuckled as he ran a finger over a page. "Mr. Wellington would probably love to see thi-"

Geri grabbed onto Laurence's sleeve and gave it a hard twist to get the Horotech's attention. "Flirt with him on your own time. Right now we got work to do."

Laurence looked like he had swallowed a bug as he blinked at Geri. "Wh-what? No I…but…I simply meant…oh…bugger..." His face turned a brilliant shade of red, which Geri ignored.

The Security Officer gave Laurence a small shake then grumbled with his face about four inches from the Horotech's. "Listen. We got a world of work to do, and not a lot of time to do it in. Any minute Smythe is going to set off whatever he's plannin' to do. If those guards fall for it, we get in, grab what we need and get out."

Laurence snapped out of his distraction with the rare book. The nod he gave Geri barely moved the cowl. He was nervous again, and growing more so by the moment now that he realized the time for the really dangerous action was upon him. He blinked a couple of times then leaned more towards the Security Officer. "And what do we do if they do not fall for it?"

Laurence could see a grim smile form on Geri's face, and the Security Officer reached into the sleeve of his robe. He pulled a plasma pistol out just far enough for Laurence to see the grip. The Horotech sucked in a sharp breath then hissed out a question. "Is that…?"

Geri nodded. "Clip full of chrono-rounds with another in my boot."

"Oh good Lord," said Laurence as he pinched the bridge of his nose under his spectacles. He wasn't certain he could bring himself to shoot priests let alone use untested chemical rounds on them.

"One way or another, we ain't coming out of this empty handed." Geri slid the pistol back up his sleeve.

A sudden shout from outside the window drew everyone's attention. A moment of confusion was shared before more shouting and cries for help could be heard followed by the unmistakable thunder of hooves. Those in the room moved to the windows to see what was going on, including one of the guards.

Geri put his hand on Laurence's shoulder and started them towards the window, but not to join the crowd. Geri was tall enough to see over those gathered at the window and he frowned at what he saw. A couple of horses were charging down the road beside the library. "That ain't gonna be near enough for what we want."

Panicked whinnies joined the shouts and screams, and the sound of running hooves multiplied as a half a dozen more horses joined their fellows to race through the streets. The guard that had gone to the window turned to call out to his partner in Italian then they both ran from the room. Geri nodded. "Okay, that will do. Come on." He turned Laurence around, and they both hurried to the restricted section.

As soon as they reached the gate Geri examined the large, iron lock that secured it. His lips pressed together then he reached into his other sleeve to pull out a small rectangular box. He opened the lid and took out a couple of slender metal rods.

Laurence had been watching the crowd to make sure they weren't being noticed. He whispered to Geri with an edge of anxiety to his voice. "What don't you have in your garb?" At the look the Security Officer gave him, Laurence held up a hand. "No. Don't tell me."

Geri chuckled as he began working on the lock with the picks. It didn't take long for a satisfying click to sound out, and the lock opened. Geri pulled the gate open and pushed Laurence through before following behind him. He pulled the gate closed again, and set the lock so that it appeared as if nothing had been tampered with. "Let's find those records."

They walked back a couple of rows of shelves, both of them eyeing the spines of the books. "How will we know when we've found the-…oh." Laurence cut himself off when he and Geri rounded a corner of shelves and took in the sight before them.

Going back deeper into the building was row upon row of dark grey leather bound books with the N and hourglass Naviwerks logo on the spines. The shelves rose above even Geri's head and seemed to go for ten yards. The lack of dust made it obvious that this section was used frequently. Geri and Laurence could only gape for a moment as they were both overwhelmed by the exact scope of information they had found.

Geri came out of it first and began to move down the rows of shelves reading spines as he went with Laurence startled into movement immediately after. Each pulled down a book at random to examine the contents, and Geri snarled quietly. "Listen to this: 'Circa 1002 Erik the Red's boat is lost and presumably sunk in the North Atlantic between Greenland and Canada. Original: Erik landed in *Vinland* and set up trade between Greenland and the Canadian natives.'"

Laurence was skimming through the entries in his own book and quoted what he found in reply. "Circa 1510. Germany. Martin Luther, monk, priest and professor of theology was found hanged in his bedchamber. The written confession found on his desk confirmed the death as suicide. Among the self-accused charges were adultery, alcohol abuse and heresy. Original: The monk nailed a letter to the door of All Saints' Church in Wittenberg, Germany 1517 that contained the Ninety Five Theses that led to the Reformation bringing about the Protestant Movement."

"What's the Protestant Movement?" Geri asked with a frown.

"I'm not sure," answered Laurence. He too wore a frown as his mind worked wildly over the possibly wide reaching effects of the alterations they had found. "But I gather that these events were important to whatever Naviwerks is plotting. Look." Laurence moved closer to Geri and held out the book with his finger pointing to an entry. "They haven't changed this one yet."

Geri peered at the book. "Original: Roderic Llançol i de Borgia becomes Pope Alexander VI, 1492." He lifted his eyes from the book to look at Laurence in astonishment. "That's why Nash is here. Now. He's setting up to alter that."

"Perhaps," said Laurence in a thoughtful tone. Then he shook his head with a scowl. "We will have to ponder this later when we have the leisure to do so." He closed the book and held it close to his chest as if guarding it. "We have to get as many of these back to *The William* as possible, and destroy the rest."

Geri looked back over his shoulder at the vast amount of ledgers. He sighed as he nodded. "They probably have copies somewhere else, but you're right. We can't leave these in one piece." He looked back to Laurence. "Got any ideas? Setting fire to 'em is too unpredictable. Could be put out before it did enough damage."

"Actually," Laurence looked up at the Security Officer with his best clever smirk, "I do. How attached are you to those chrono-rounds?"

Geri pulled back with a disapproving expression. "What?"

Laurence held up a hand in a pacifying gesture

and sent up a silent prayer that the Security Officer wouldn't knock him over the head for his impertinence. "The chemicals that those rounds contain are highly unstable if mistreated. Sealed and stored the way they are they no doubt do not have a reaction until the casing cracks under pressure. However, when exposed to a variable-…"

"Skip the science lesson and make your point." Geri glared at Laurence.

"Ah. Right." Laurence grimaced then swallowed against a throat gone dry for that look. "Recall, if you will, that I work with these chemicals all of the time in engineering. I can make them react however I like. In this case, I am thinking an implosion."

Geri's brows twitched upward. Laurence hoped that meant he had impressed the Security Officer. "Will that do it or just bury the books?"

Laurence nodded. "The chemicals are not meant to-…" he broke off when Geri gave him another menacing look. "Yes. It will destroy the books."

Geri gave a single, tight nod then pulled the pistol out of his sleeve. He ejected the clip, grabbed Laurence by the wrist and slapped it into the Horotech's palm. "Do it." His robe was hitched up so he could retrieve the clip from his boot and he gave that one to Laurence as well. "I'll hail *The William*. Tell them we'll need a speedy pick-up. How long do you need?"

"Ah," Laurence had to put a clip on a shelf in order to figure out how to pop the bullets out. "*I am a technical engineer, damn it!*" he mentally chastised himself. *"I can unload a silly gun clip."* Audibly, he addressed Geri. "How much time do you want? I can rig a delay."

"Ten minutes, tops," was Geri's reply. At Laurence's nod he triggered the voice activation to the comm unit in his ear then began grabbing random books into his arm. "Reynolds to Flynn. We're gonna need a touch and go outside the library. E.T.A. ten minutes. Priority Confetti."

Laurence looked up from where he was wrapping a length of copper wire around the clip he hadn't unloaded. He looked at Geri and mouthed the word *confetti* with a quizzical look on his face. Geri shook his head at him as he pointed at the bullets.

"Roger that, Reynolds." Angel's voice could be heard through their ear comm units, which spurred Laurence into swifter action. *"Pick up in the Papal Gardens. Ten minutes. Explosion pending"*

Geri went back to loading up his arm with books while Laurence continued to set up a makeshift bomb. After a few minutes, Geri was beside the Horotech looking at what he'd done. "Looks like all you did was string 'em up together like Christmas lights."

"Pretty much exactly," said Laurence in a distracted voice. He was sprinkling some powder over a strand of the metal wire from a tube. Satisfied with the amount, he replaced the stopper in the tube, and tucked it away under his robe. "Mr. Reynolds, I wonder if you would be so kind as to scout the swiftest escape route to the Papal Gardens from our current location?" His voice was calm, but there was a slight edge to it that got through to Geri.

"…shit." Geri cautiously slid around Laurence then rushed back down the row of shelves leaving Laurence to whatever he was going to do with that small bottle of liquid, and the strip of cloth he was inserting into it.

Not a minute later Laurence all but ran into his back. "Do we have an exit strategy, because now would be the opportune time to make use of it."

"Uh," muttered Geri, as he looked towards the gate then further back in the restricted section. Some narrow windows could be seen high on a wall. "Through the gate would be too long. We'd have to go around the building." He nodded towards the windows. "If I don't miss my guess the garden is just out there."

"Right." For once Laurence did not display any sort of hesitation. He grabbed Geri's sleeve and started jogging through the rows towards the windows, which fortunately faced away from the direction of his little bomb, which was what had made up his mind.

The shelves were a veritable labyrinth but without dead ends; with the windows streaming daylight they were easy guides. They came out from an aisle to find themselves with an open area and a clear line of sight on the windows, but a flash of bronze in a sunbeam caught their attention. Both men stared for a moment then looked at each other.

"You have got to be kidding me," said Geri, his arms full of ledgers.

*****

Captain Alex burst onto the bridge with as much force as she could while using a cane. Her pale blue eyes were snapping with the anxiety coursing through her. Dr. Hennessey hadn't been given any choice but to follow her as soon as they heard Angel's report over the internal comms. She knew better than to make assumptions until she had all of the information, but Geri would not have used the code word he had if things weren't desperate.

Angel had kept *The William's Hunt* in the upper atmosphere to avoid being seen by anachronistic eyes, but she had begun a descent at Captain Alex's command. It made navigating with the cane more of a challenge, but she would not allow a little thing like increasing gravity and pitch get in her way. She even took the short lattice ironwork stairs without the assistance of the cane. Her eyes trained immediately on the heads up steam screen.

"Report," she said as she made for the captain's chair with a hurried limp.

"We'll be landing in the Papal Gardens. E.T.A three minutes." Angel replied with only slight distraction. She was busy going back and forth from toggle to switch to control their drop. "There's some kind of hubbub in the area, but I don't think it's our guys."

"Show me," ordered Captain Alex.

Angel looked to the overhead display as she turned a knob that would enhance the external visual. "On screen." Immediately they could see the stampede of horses.

Nigel came to stand next to the helm and snorted as he crossed his arms. "Oh, I don't know. Those horses might have gotten a look at our good Mr. Reynolds."

Captain Alex didn't bother replying to her Historian. Some sort of explosion was in the offing, and she would feel much better about it if they had a visual on her landside team. "Belay the standing protocol, Miss Flynn. Steady as she goes." Her expression turned grim as she sat in her chair. Her hand came to rest on the pommel of the sabre where it rested in the stays to her right. She purposely didn't clench her fingers around the hilt not wanting to give away her tension level.

Dr. Hennessey took up position behind her chair while Nigel and Angel exchanged a quick glance. There were probably going to be historical reports and paintings with sightings of their ship after this, but no one dared question the Captain's order. Angel just kept the heading steady.

Finally, the Holy See compound could be seen through the windows. It was still too far away for Alex's peace of mind, but they were coming in swiftly. It took every ounce of self-control that she had not to get up out of her seat, but her jaw was clenched tightly together, and her fingers drummed against the arm of her chair.

The buildings increased in size as they steadily grew closer until details of people rushing to catch the horses could be picked out along with the images in the stained glass windows.

"Landing procedure engaged." Angel took the wheel with one hand while the other pulled a lever down its slot. A moment later a sudden vibration announced a successful lowering of the landing gear.

"What is that?" Nigel asked. He frowned in curiosity as he moved around the helm towards the front windshield to get a better look. Something had crashed through the glass of a tall narrow window that faced the Garden. "Is that…Mr. Kane?" he asked incredulously.

"What?" Captain Alex didn't have to ask Angel to focus on the side of the building. Her Pilot just made the visual adjustment and the view on the steam screen zoomed in to show Laurence with his arms full of books tumbling out of the window. He got tangled in his monk's robe as he tried to stand and juggle the books at the same time. Then they saw Geri appear in the window. He slapped an arm against the outside of the building, but he seemed to have trouble squeezing his chest through sideways.

He appeared to have made it, but no one could be sure since the screen filled with a blinding flash. Nigel's hand pressed against the forward window as that wing of the library suddenly collapsed in on itself sending a cloud of dust and debris into the air thick enough to obscure sight.

Captain Alex's eyes went wide as she lurched out of her chair and cried out, "***GERI!***"

Come About

XI
From the Rubble

As Angel Flynn landed the ship in the Papal Garden, the eyes of Captain Alex, Nigel, and Dr. Hennessey were trained solidly on the cloud of dust that obscured the view of the wing of the Vatican Library. They had just watched it implode as Laurence Kane and Geri Reynolds scrambled to escape the building through a narrow window; the last they knew both men were well within the blast radius. As debris rained down against the hull of *The William's Hunt*, what remained of her crew was desperate for a sign of life.

Smoke joined the dust cloud, adding to Captain Alex's mounting frustration. Fires had apparently broken out amongst the rubble. The only saving grace was that the few native people who were still in the area were more concerned with getting to anyone injured by the destruction rather than taking notice of an extremely out of place chrono-ship.

Alex only took notice of this fact peripherally as her eyes scanned for her missing crew members. As more time ticked by, the less likely it became that Laurence and Geri would walk out of that slowly diminishing cloud. Her heart beat fiercely against her chest as worry and guilt vied for rule within her. Geri was used to such situations, but that wasn't to say she enjoyed putting him at such risk. As for Laurence, she dearly hoped she hadn't gotten her Horotech killed or severely injured on his first run with her.

After what seemed like an eternity, Angel sat up abruptly in her chair and pointed out the forward window. "Look!" She adjusted the view on the steam screen making the image swim back and forth until she got it focused on what her keen eyes had picked out in the settling cloud. Two silhouettes could be seen moving in their direction.

Captain Alex stepped closer towards the steam screen, her expression tense. Dr. Hennessey was a few paces behind her while Nigel was so close to the forward window his nose touched the glass. A sound of relief came from Alex as all of them saw Laurence and Geri step into sight. The laughter started with Nigel, but bubbled forth from everyone on the bridge when they saw the grins the two men were wearing.

Alex clapped her hands together once. Her laughter edged on manic for the relief she felt as she walked back to her captain's chair. She sat back down before her knees buckled out from beneath her. Sprawling in the chair, she rubbed her fingers at her forehead. Dr. Hennessey watched her with a controlled smile on his face. Either she didn't realize that she had cried out Geri's name, or didn't care that the others heard her. She would never admit to either, but when she noticed

Dr. Hennessey looking at her, she smiled in return with a nod of her head.

"Cap!" Angel brought Alex's attention back to the helm. "Look what Mr. Reynolds has."

Alex's brows creased downward as she peered at the steam screen then let out with another abrupt laugh. "He has that damn model."

"And our good Mr. Kane is not without his share of swag." Nigel chuckled as he walked away from the front windshield. "Something for me, perhaps. The chap is coming around, I think."

Captain Alex gave her Historian a bland smirk as she stood up from her chair once more. "Miss Flynn, get us in the air as soon as they are on board. Find an unpopulated space to circle. The rest of you come with me." She turned for the latticework staircase leading out of the bridge.

"Aye, Cap," called Angel as she checked her control console. After a brief look she glanced back over her shoulder. "Tell them I said welcome back, 'k?"

Alex looked back to her Pilot from the landing, her delicate hands resting on the railing. She smiled to Angel and gave her a nod before stepping out of the bridge to go find out just what in Hell her landside crew had done.

******

By the time Alex, Nigel, and Dr. Hennessey were exiting the lift into the hold, Angel had the ship in the air. As they stepped off the lift, they could smell the burned chemicals that permeated Geri and Laurence's monks' garb. Captain Alex wrinkled her nose a little as she led the other two towards the staging area where her returning crew members were stripping off the offending garments. She wasn't aware the slight limp caused by the injury in her side had returned, but she had managed to regain a stoic expression during the ride down. There was even a hint of a pleased smirk at the corners of her lips.

"I say." Nigel walked past Captain Alex with an open smile for Laurence and Geri as he pushed his long fingers through his fashionably tussled hair. "If that was an example of what we can expect from you two then I shall have the good Doctor prescribe me some laudanum."

Laurence's blush made him look five years younger than normal. That was impressive since he already looked younger than his twenty-seven years, but his sheepish grin and rumpled hair just added to the effect. "Well ah…it wasn't precisely how we would have liked for-…"

"Get over it, Wellington." Geri interrupted Laurence with a proud smirk on his craggy face. "It worked, didn't it?"

"At the cost of a historical building," came Captain Alex's quiet but stern voice. She arched a brow at her Security Officer, but it did nothing to diminish Geri's expression.

"Your pardon, Captain." Laurence surprised them all by stepping forward to draw the Captain's attention to him. His spectacles had been jarred when he had taken off the monk's robes, and he straightened them as he addressed her. "Father Smythe told us that wing of the library was due for reconstruction anyway." He glanced at Geri warily but with a smile still hovering on his lips. "We simply…helped things along."

To surprise her even more, Geri moved up next to Laurence, and put his large hand on the Horotech's shoulder. The look he gave his Captain was confident and proud. "The kid did good, Captain."

"And what exactly would it be that you did, Mr. Kane?" Alex wasn't quite ready to let either of them entirely off the hook. While all of them were considered rogues at the very least for going against the only approved authority in time traveling, she was still a firm proponent of a non-interference policy while visiting the past. It was bad enough that she had tossed certain protocols out the window for this job.

"I uh…" Laurence looked to Geri whose hand was still on his shoulder. At the encouraging nod he was given he turned back to Captain Alex with a meek smile. "I ignited all of Mr. Reynolds' chrono-rounds to create a singularity small enough to avoid opening a wormhole of significance. Making use of the gunpowder within the bullets and a little phosphorus, I overheated the chemicals. That reaction combined with the singularity caused the building to implode rather than explode which is also why Mr. Reynolds and I are relatively unscathed from the experience." He smiled, rather proud of himself. "We were far enough away to not get sucked into the reaction, but I will admit a certain amount of anxiety on my part at the time." A nervous laugh escaped him, which made Nigel grin.

"Glad you're on our side," said Geri as he hugged Laurence's head with one arm.

Alex looked from one man to the other. At the beginning of this, she hadn't been certain any one of her crew would have warmed to Laurence. The mousy Horotech had little experience on a crew and few social graces. Nigel certainly appreciated Laurence's appearance, but she hadn't been willing to commit to anything more than her Historian trying to make Laurence twitch. The fact that Geri was giving Laurence a glowing compliment in front of witnesses didn't just speak volumes for his opinion of the smaller man. It screamed it.

"I see," she said quietly. She could feel Dr. Hennessey behind her as well as Nigel's eyes on her as they waited to see how she handled this. Her pale blue eyes landed solidly on Laurence, which made him shift in place under her scrutiny. "Well done then, Mr. Kane." She allowed him to see a small smile of approval as she nodded to him.

Her attention then went to the stack of ledgers Laurence had kept tucked in his arm. "That is the information Fillion said we needed to find, I take it?" She quickly picked out the faded embossed lettering on the spine. The Naviwerks logo was difficult to miss, but she got a sinking feeling upon reading the numbers beneath it. If she didn't miss her guess, those were dates in blocks of centuries per ledger.

"It is, Captain," said Laurence in a gentle voice. His expression sobered as he reverently handed the stack of four books to Captain Alex. "Although I rather doubt that their contents will be very reassuring."

Alex reached for the books but Dr. Hennessey stepped forward to take them before she could. He gave her a pointed look as he handed the ledgers to Nigel. "Wellington can bring these to you soon enough when we are resting comfortably in our own berths."

Alex gave the Doctor a sour look, but she wasn't going to argue with him in front of the rest of the crew. Besides, she could feel the wound in her side throbbing. The fast track meds were working, but she had pushed it, and she needed to get off her feet. She silently promised Abraham that she would do just that… in a moment. She looked back to Geri and nodded to the bronze statue resting on one of the supply crates. "Would you care to explain that, Mr. Reynolds?"

Geri let out with a snort as he picked up the foot and a half tall horse. "Looks to me as if you should be askin' Wellington for explanations, Captain not me." He bounced the model in his hand as he arched a brow at Nigel.

"Oh, I say!" exclaimed Nigel. He gave the Security Officer a scowl as he pulled a stylus and note pad from his inner coat pocket. The frame for the memory pad had been decorated with paisley fabrics and paper passages from books the Historian had a particular taste for, all of which had been carefully lacquered onto the metal. "All of the references I found suggested a four foot model. As did the contract, I might add." The stylus slid across the light screen rapidly as he skimmed through his notes on the Gran Cavallo. He paused with a blink on one page then enlarged the image with his fingers and hummed thoughtfully. "Oh dear." An apologetic smile formed on his face, which he turned upon Captain Alex. "It seems there is a faded tick next to the fraction indicating the model was one *sixteenth* the size, not one sixth."

Dr. Hennessey looked over Nigel's shoulder at

the image on the note pad screen then nodded. "Very faded. Easy mistake, old chap." He patted Nigel on the back before stepping back.

"So this is the actual model then?" asked Captain Alex. She tried not to show the hope she was feeling just in case the model was a fake.

Nigel sucked in a breath as he hesitated to answer. He looked at Geri who had tucked the model under his arm then made a vague gesture with his arm. "Without any other proof to contradict it, the model *was* found in the Vatican Library where it was said to have been taken." He gave Captain Alex a weak smile. "My opinion is yes. This is the working model of Leonardo da Vinci's Gran Cavallo."

A pleased grin spread across Captain Alex's face. What had seemed like a failed contract had worked in their favor after all. They were going to get paid! Even if she had to call the museum curator out on the doublecross. There was nothing like a little intimidation to make someone sweeten the pot. Besides, she was certain she could sell the model to another museum if need be. "Excellent." Her voice sounded stronger than it had since she had been shot outside of Milan. "Mr. Reynolds, secure that swag. Mr. Wellington, Dr. Hennessey, get to your quarters and batten down your areas. Mr. Kane! Report to engineering. We are going home." Orders given, she turned for the lift with less of a hitch in her stride than when she had arrived in the hold. A satisfying end to their maiden voyage obviously did wonders for her stamina.

Nigel and Dr. Hennessey followed along with her exchanging good-natured banter while Geri and

Laurence hung back for a moment. Geri had what for him was a pleasant smile on his face as he watched Captain Alex enter the lift with that slight limp.

Laurence thought he saw something wistful in the Security Officer's eyes, and put his hand on the man's broad shoulders. "We all heard it, my friend."

Geri's smile disappeared, but he didn't look at the Horotech. "Heard what?"

Laurence, as socially inept as he was, didn't pick up on the subtle suggestion to drop the subject. "We heard the Captain call out your name. When the library imploded." He offered a weak smile to the Security Officer as he removed the comm link from his ear. It was obvious, even to Laurence, that there were tender feelings between Geri and Captain de Sade. It occurred to him that her retreat back into her stoic and cold demeanor was an attempt on her part to hide them. That couldn't have settled well with Geri, he assumed. Laurence knew he might very well be overstepping the companionship that he and Geri seemed to have developed during their recent experiences, but when he considered somebody a friend he didn't back down. He did expect the brush off, however.

But to Laurence's surprise, Geri let out a breath through his nose, his eyes still trained on the empty lift shaft, and clapped a hand to the Horotech's shoulder. His expression was flat, which was a far cry better than his typical scowl. "Best get to work." Then without another word he plucked up the Gran Cavallo model then walked away to secure it in one of the many crates.

"Cap?" Angel's voice came over the internal comm speakers just as Laurence had entered the lift,

and Captain Alex, Nigel and Dr. Hennessey were returning to their respective quarters. *"Sensors indicate a wormhole activation within ten miles."*

Captain Alex froze in place for a single moment with her eyes widening, then rushed to the squawk box that was on the wall by the stairs leading to the Mess Hall. She almost tore the mic from its brass cradle on the side of the plain redwood box in her haste. Depressing the button with her thumb, she brought the mic right up to her lips and gave the handle a hard crank to activate the broadcast function. "All hands to their stations double time. Mr. Kane, prepare for immediate return through the wormhole. Mr. Reynolds to the bridge. Captain de Sade out." She slammed the mic into its housing before she raced up the stairs taking two at a time.

Dr. Hennessey cursed softly under his breath. He was going to end up re-stitching that bullet hole when this was all over. He gave Nigel a push. "Go on, son. I have a feeling this is going to get bumpy."

XII
Confrontation

Captain Alex burst through the door of the bridge with an intense expression. "Was it coming or going, Miss Flynn?" she asked as she hurried down the short flight of stairs. Her pale blue eyes scanned over the displays she could see, as her Pilot was in the process of prepping the ship for the return to their own time. Chemical steam hissed through piping overhead as the fuel was shared between the thrust ports and the chrono-engine. Old habit forced her to look over the copper pipes, brass brackets and C-clamps to ensure there were no leaks. Not finding any, she turned her attention back to the helm.

"Returning, Cap," Angel replied without looking up from her consoles. Deft fingers turned a knob, and the steam screen displayed the readings the sensors had picked up. "They weren't even trying to hide it."

Alex moved towards the Captain's chair with purposeful strides as she took in the readings. Sure enough, the energy signatures registered as a return instead of an arrival, which would have given off a much more powerful signature due to the amount of energy needed to punch a hole through time. "Nash went home." She sat in her chair with her eyes narrowing as she idly tied her thick, dark auburn hair back into a ponytail.

Angel glanced back at her Captain and did a bit of a double take. "Seems that way. Expecting trouble, Cap?" She raised her brows before looking back to her controls.

"Always, Miss Flynn." Alex knew why Angel had asked her that. The only time she pulled her hair back if she had already left it loose was if she was going to need it out of the way quickly. It was an old habit from when she was learning how to fence. Angel recognized the gesture, and Alex saw no reason to deny what she anticipated. "I do not trust that the decoy marker worked as well as planned."

In an attempt to throw off Naviwerks' sensors from picking up chrono activity when *The William's Hunt's* chrono-engine activated, Captain Alex had ordered Laurence to give a minuscule charge of the engine, effectively dropping a marker that Alex had hoped would distract the corporation. The theory was sound, but it had never been put into practical use. She didn't want to take any chances.

Geri arrived on the bridge and immediately took note of Captain Alex's hair. "We expectin' trouble?" he asked as he came down the stairs.

Alex pointed towards the monitoring station as she answered her Security Officer. "Take visuals, Mr. Reynolds. I want eyes fore and aft." She paused for just a moment as Geri immediately followed her order. "The activation was a return. I'm expecting a welcoming party." She and Geri exchanged a quick knowing look then he was switching on the external imaging.

Monitors lit up around Geri showing nothing more than the fifteenth century skies around them. Captain Alex ignored them temporarily in lieu of opening the comm channel to Engineering. "Mr. Kane, what is your status?"

The speakers on the bridge clicked to indicate that Laurence had switched to voice activated mode on his end before his voice came through. *"We have a full charge, Captain. Ready for return."*

"Standby, Mr. Kane." Captain Alex closed the connection as she looked to the back of Angel's head. "Miss Flynn. On my mark I want you to give me a full burn."

The order was strange enough to make Angel turn her chair to look at her Captain in confusion. "That won't do us any good in the hole, Cap. Propulsion is nothing more than a waste of fuel during transit."

"I am well aware of that, thank you." Captain Alex's voice and expression were flint sharp. "Full burn. On my mark, please."

"Aye, Cap," said Angel before she turned back around. She glanced at Geri as she adjusted the controls for a full burn of the engines. He gave her a shrug in return. The shake of her head was barely noticeable as she turned her attention back to the consoles.

Alex's dainty fingers tapped on the control panel in the arm of her chair, turning on the comm again. "Mr. Kane. Activate the return." A flick of a digit put the comm channel to broadband so she could address the rest of her crew. “Everyone strap in.” After closing the channel, she heeded her own command and pulled her harness over her shoulders. The click of the connectors engaging was followed shortly by the sounds of Geri and Angel doing the same.

“Aye, Captain.” Laurence’s voice acknowledged Captain Alex’s order, and the ship seemed to lurch as the chrono-engine reversed itself, pulling them back into the wormhole they had come through. It hadn’t really put the ship into reverse. It was just a trick of the senses that suggested the ship had changed direction.

The sky disappeared, once more replaced with the over-bright whiteness and the twinkling pinpoints of light that darted and spiraled around the ship as it passed through the wormhole. This time however, Captain Alex did not watch the display. Instead, her gaze was glued to the ornate clock on the wall of the bridge, its hands frozen on eleven fifteen and thirty two seconds. Her fingers hovered over the chair controls to initiate the full burn. It wasn’t that she didn’t trust Angel to follow the order, but what she had in mind required instant reaction. A single hesitation and it would be all for naught.

Her all too pale eyes were unblinking as she stared at that clock. Her teeth were clenched together and her lips were parted just a little bit. Tension filled the bridge as moments seemed to pass by at a snail’s pace. Any other captain might fill these moments with thoughts of alternate plans should the first fail. Not Captain Alex. She had every confidence in the crazy stunt she had in mind and strong faith in her crew to help her pull it off. It was that one, remote chance that the timing would be off, and this could all go south that made the tendons in her neck stand out.

Her focus narrowed onto the second hand of the clock as her lips moved silently. Then any doubt became moot as the hand gave a single tock. Alex's eyes widened as she barked out, "Now!"

She should not have doubted her Pilot's ability to follow through. Angel's hand mashed down on the thruster button just as the dizzying images created by the wormhole melted away to normal, blue sky. The engines ignited in the returned atmosphere, and *The William's Hunt* shot forward…

…right between two Naviwerks ships.

Angel laughed full out while Geri's grin matched the one their Captain wore. "Now *that* was beautiful, Cap!" Angel called out as her hands wrapped around the steering. They all knew that the ships would come after them, but it would take a moment or two. No one expected anyone to be mad enough to come blasting out of a wormhole at a full burn. There was typically no need, nor was there a predictable way to judge how long a ship would remain in a wormhole. Except Captain Alex had just done that.

"Now we know why you always have an analog clock on the bridge, Captain." Geri smirked at Alex as he gave her a curt nod.

"Digital clocks never stop when going through a wormhole, Mr. Reynolds." Alex's voice held her amusement. "Just analog. Nobody is certain why, but that is why Naviwerks never uses them. A lazy captain can keep track of the days with a digital clock, and not miss their five day window." She chuckled as she looked back up at the clock. She had never used it for something like this before, but she was very grateful now for that seemingly random habit she had developed.

"Two bogeys in pursuit, Captain." Geri's announcement brought their attention back to him. Sure enough, in the aft monitor, the two Naviwerks chrono-ships could be seen in a full burn after them.

"Prepare for evasive maneuvers, Miss Flynn." Alex felt a thrill rush through her, but was glad that her excitement did not translate through to her tone of voice. She sounded as calm as ever as she gave the order.

"Aye, Cap," answered Angel as she flipped the toggle on her console from automatic to manual navigation. It gave her full control.

The rapid buzzing of a bell filled the bridge before Angel pushed a button, muting it. "We're being hailed, Cap."

Captain Alex had been expecting it, and got an eager smirk on her face. "Put it on screen."

Angel nodded as she turned a knob to the Send/Receive position, flipped a switch to open the connection, and then Agent Nash's grim face filled the steam screen. It was obvious that he'd had time to change out of period clothing and into his pristine Naviwerks uniform, a Tier 2 Agent insignia on his shoulder. His dirty blonde hair was short and neat. The scar on his left cheek was clearly visible along with the irritation in his dark blue eyes. His voice carried over the speakers with its lack of intonation. *"Alex."*

Geri frowned more than usual upon seeing Nash again. His arms and neck tightened in response to his anger, but Alex held a hand out towards him, gesturing him to silence.

Nash hadn't given her any rank, but Alex hadn't expected him to. She felt a stab of sad nostalgia for seeing him; the last time she had spoken with Nash had been just before she made her decision to leave Naviwerks. He had been so excited and proud since he had known the corporation had offered her a promotion. The pain she had felt then for being forced into the decision to leave him echoed within her now, but it was overshadowed by a growing horror. Stoic they both may have been, but he had never seemed so lifeless before. Something was wrong.

Alex kept her emotions deeply hidden; none of them would serve her at this moment. Instead, she put on a cold, if polite, smile as she replied. "Hello, Eldon." She purposely made her tone of voice conversational as if they had just crossed paths on the way to the grocers' and were about to catch up.

"His name is Eldon?" Angel hissed out an amused whisper to Geri who smirked at her as he nodded his head.

"Alexandria de Sade," said Nash with a stern expression. *"It is my duty as an Agent of Naviwerks to inform you that you are in violation of a variety of Chrono-Regulations as agreed upon by the Murdock Initiatives of-..."*

Captain Alex cut him off. "I'm not an employee of Naviwerks anymore, Eldon." She still maintained that casual tone of voice with that plastic smile in place. "The Initiatives no longer apply. As well you know."

"Then how about the law, Alex?" Nash was growing more irritated as proven by the small tick that made the scar on his cheek jump. *"You are in possession of stolen property."*

"I am?" The look of absolute surprise and innocence that Alex affected made Geri choke back a laugh. The petite hand gracefully placed to her chest didn't help. "I see no serial numbers. Nor any Naviwerks logos. And," she drew that word out a little, "our last diagnostic revealed no corporate connections established by their systems." Alex dropped the act to give Nash a narrow eyed smile. "*The William's Hunt* belongs to me."

Angel grinned to Geri who gave her a wink, but both kept quiet as Nash raised his voice.

"Damn it, Alex! I am trying to help you before you take things too far." His eyes had widened, with his pupils visibly dilating.

"Help me how, Eldon?" Alex sprawled a little in her Captain's chair, and put her chin in her hand. "We are both familiar with Naviwerks' form of justice. No law in any nation can touch them so they police their own as laid out in those same Initiatives you wish to bind me by." She let out a dramatic sigh. "I am afraid I have no interest in either being abandoned in some backwater point in history or installed with a brand new form of neural control."

Her pale blue eyes locked onto Nash through the steam screen. He gave away no surprise, no reaction at all, and while he had never been demonstrative, he hadn't been this cold either. His lack of expression confirmed to Alex's mind that he had undergone the nano-therapies. She felt her heart break a little more.

"Then you give me no choice." Nash's voice lost all hint of emotion. *"You and your crew will be brought to the board to face judgment."*

"And how do you see that happening?" Alex straightened herself in her chair and arched a brow at Nash with a haughty expression. Her hand came to rest on her chair. Her finger brushed against the touch screen control set into the arm, triggering a silent alert to Angel. Her Pilot disengaged the alert to indicate that she had received it, and was ready.

"You have been flying without refueling for days now." Nash smiled but it was a cold, smug expression. *"It's only a matter of time before we overtake you and attach tow lines."*

Captain Alex laughed which made Nash frown. "Oh, Eldon." She shook her head as she let her chuckle dwindle away. "Everybody knows that I'm the better captain. Remember? I had the best fuel charts in the company." Her eyes sparkled as she gave Nash a challenging smile. "Catch me if you can."

Her finger tapped the control in the arm of her chair to disengage the transmission just before she turned to Angel and Geri. "Report."

"Bogeys closing, Captain," replied Geri immediately. He smirked at Alex. "As expected."

Captain Alex smiled with a grim look in her eyes. "You have the helm, Miss Flynn. Do us proud."

Angel grinned as she laced her fingers together then forced her palms forward to pop her knuckles.

"Aye, Cap." Her grin remained as she wrapped her fingers one by one around the wheel.

Alex checked her harness straps to make certain they were secure. The bumpy ride was going to get a little bumpier soon. She knew they would have to make an impression when they encountered Naviwerks, and had even assumed it would be Nash they would face. She and some of her crew had prepared for just this moment.

"Their tow line ports are opening," Geri said. "I have the mark."

Angel nodded as she popped a stick of gum into her mouth.

"And…" Geri lifted his hand up then dropped it quickly. "Mark!"

Angel's gum snapped as she cut the engines and shoved the wheel forward. It forced the directional flaps into a vertical position and gravity took effect. The ship dropped abruptly, which allowed the grappling lines the Naviwerks ships fired at *The William's Hunt* to pass right overhead.

"Hold on to something," warned Angel then she threw the ignition switch. The whine of the engine turbines coming back online was almost ominous while the ship was in freefall. She jostled the choke up and down to prime the fuel, and for a moment, a doubt hung in the air. But the engines ignited when she pressed the thruster button, and Angel put them into a full burn as she hauled the wheel back. *The William* bucked once before she leveled out and shot forward at top speed.

"Mr. Reynolds?" Captain Alex's voice was a bit clipped. That and the whites of her knuckles on the arms of her chair were the only indications of her apprehension. Otherwise, she appeared just as calm as ever.

Geri checked the aft and above monitors before a smug look came to his face. “Bogeys are slowed down, Captain. Tow lines swayin’ in the breeze.”

A pleased smile formed on Alex’s face as she turned to her Pilot. “Well done, Miss Flynn. Stay the course.”

“Aye, Cap!” Angel was grinning around her gum, obviously having a splendid time.

The bell buzzed a warning again, and Captain Alex chuckled as Angel muted it. “Patch him through, Miss Flynn.” Angel flicked the switch with a roll of her eyes that only Geri caught.

Alex wasn’t going to allow Nash to have the first word again, so as soon as his face appeared in the steam screen she smiled brightly. “Eldon! Are you still back there? You should go home. You look tired.”

Nash looked furious. *“I am only going to offer this once, Alexandria. Surrender your vessel now, and I give you my word that we will go lightly on your crew.*

Alex gave a delicate snort of derision then leaned forward, impossibly light blue eyes locking with his dark blues. “With all due respect, you go to Hell.”

“Do not be foolish. This is a generous offer.” Nash was all but snarling at her.

“That is a matter of opinion,” Alex said as she looked at Geri and gave him a nod. Her Security Officer got up from the monitoring station with the happiest grin anyone may have ever seen on his face, then darted off to leave the bridge.

Captain Alex looked back to Nash, and all amusement left her expression. "Now hear my offer. Withdraw your ships. Call off your hunt, or I will consider my hand to be forced."

Nash's eyes narrowed as he grit his teeth. *"You are but one ship while I can summon an armada. You can only run for so long."*

There wasn't a hint of mercy to be seen in Nash. If Alex needed more proof that whatever they had between them was now firmly in past, the look on his face was it. She felt something within her cry out then fade. It left behind a cold, hollow place near her heart that showed through her eyes. Nash obviously noticed it, but you had to know him as well as Alex did to recognize what that blink he gave meant.

She lifted her chin with an arrogant look settling upon her features as her finger pressed against the panel set into the arm of her chair. "So be it."

*****

Geri had run out of the bridge on Captain Alex's silent order. He had honestly been looking forward to this. He would get to play with his new toy! On a normal schematic for a chrono-ship there was only a short hallway that led from the bridge to the stairs, down to Mess and up to Engineering. Geri and Alex had made a modification, which he took after he left the bridge. He reached out with a hand and grabbed a rung of the ladder they had attached to the wall right off of the stairs from the bridge. He swung his momentum around and planted a boot on another rung to propel himself up the new ladder.

It led to the next addition he and Captain Alex

had made in preparation for a confrontation with Naviwerks. After working for the corporation for as long as he had in the Security Corp he knew how organized they were, as well as their potential for ruthlessness. He and Captain Alex had put their heads together over a few pints, and came up with a radical new design for the ship. He had a few contacts under the radar, damn near underground actually, and one of them with military connections had come through for him.

His hand encountered the trapdoor he'd fabricated into the inner frame that buffered the hull and created a crawl space. He'd had to be a little creative in getting around the chemi-steam pipes and wiring that fed through the ship to make room for the turret he pulled himself into, but he had managed it. It was a tight squeeze for his bulk, or would be until he raised the turret and was able to lower the M60D machine gun he had bolted to the floor into firing position.

Geri pushed the large button on the wall of the turret with his fist before he slid into the gunner's seat, and a hatch opened in the hull to allow the turret to rise up and out of the ship. As he waited for position to be achieved, he pulled the stub of a cigar from the pocket of his shirt and jammed it between his teeth at the corner of his mouth. Ammo feed looked good, the straps to the seat were secure, and as soon as he was able, he pulled on the twin grips to lower the barrel of the gun through the slot designed for it in the metal and bolt framed glass of the turret. His left thumb toggled on the steam powered turbine that would feed the rounds through as he fired, and he cock-checked the loader. Then he grinned as he sighted on the two Naviwerks ships behind *The William's Hunt.* All he waited on now was Captain Alex's green light.

Literally. He had wired in a pair of lights, one green, one red. It would be impossible to hear commands over a comm with the gun operational. The light system would allow the Captain to give him Go and Stop orders.

It came a few moments later. The green light flared to life. Geri's right thumb pressed the firing button on the handle and he opened upon the Naviwerks ship on the right. Armor piercing rounds sprayed in an almost perfect line.

*****

The machine gun firing was more felt than heard in the bridge. Captain Alex hadn't closed the line between *The William's Hunt* and Nash. She had wanted to see his reaction to the modification that had been made to one of their precious chrono-ships. What she saw satisfied her.

Nash had turned to bark orders as the other ship took damage from Geri's new toy. *"Veer off! Evasive maneuvers!"* There was a pause from him when his Pilot shouted something back to him that couldn't be understood over the comm link. It became apparent however with Nash's angry reply that they did not possess a Pilot as talented as Angel. *"Then engage the manual override! Disengage pursuit or be shot down, you idiot!"*

Captain Alex chuckled under her breath before she smiled to Nash with a calm demeanor designed to annoy him. "Having a problem with your Pilots, Eldon?" She had not yet given the command to cease fire.

She could see by the exterior monitors that Geri continued to shoot at the two ships following *The William's Hunt.* The turret was able to swivel 360 degrees, and as long as Naviwerks was still within range, there was no chance for them to avoid being shot. Geri stopped however when the two chrono-ships changed course abruptly, breaking off pursuit. One of them was trailing a steam cloud that vented from the bottom starboard. Geri knew where the ships were vulnerable and had made a point when the warning shots hadn't made an adequate impression.

Nash turned back to Alex, his face a mask of fury. *"What have you done?! A gun, Alex? Which you fired upon unarmed ships? How far have you slipped from that moral code you were so proud of?"*

"Not as far as you." Alex's voice was cold with her accusation. "What have *you* done, Eldon? What have you allowed them to do to you?" Her teeth clenched together as her lip curled upward in disgust. "You are no longer the man I knew, and as you said, we are but one ship while you have an armada. My moral code hasn't altered its course. I simply armed it." She was beginning to tire of the whole encounter, and it was starting to show in the tone of her voice. It was time to end the conversation.

Angel glanced back at Alex who lifted a finger and pointed at the Pilot. "Go back to Naviwerks, Eldon. Tell them they have competition now, and we will not abide their hypocrisy. *The William's Hunt* has the ROW."

That being her cue, Angel tapped out a command on her comm station then Nash's face on the steam screen was replaced with the white skull and crossed swords on a black field insignia once flown by Captain Calico Jack Rackham, whose ship Captain Alex honored in the name of her own. The signal did not just serve to mock Agent Nash and the company he represented, but it contained a hidden code that scrambled their Navigation systems and fuel sensors. Not only would they not know which direction they were flying in, but also their fuel would be delivered at a bare minimum making a full burn impossible. At least long enough for Angel to get *The William's Hunt* out of visual range and distance collapsed the communications link.

Epilogue

Warm, low lighting from electric bulbs designed to simulate the look of gas flames emanated from brass sconces on the dark wood panels that divided the plain rose-colored wallpaper. The quiet hiss of steam through the iron radiators was overpowered by the scratch of the Victrola needle against a pressed vinyl disc as she turned the crank on the side of the box to set the turntable spinning. Her lithe fingers picked up the crystal snifter that sat next to the music box, and brought it to her lips for a sip of the fine, aged cognac within. She walked away just as a piano chord clinked out the measure four times sharply then repeated the beat in a single chord progression. The musician repeated this before a drum beat began, and it was all joined by a bass and a clarinet that established a haunting melody. By the time she draped herself on the fainting couch another piano plinked out the downbeat with notes in a lower octave.

"Hey babe, where'd you say you were goin'?

Goin' down the street to see Delicious Cabaret." Captain Alexandria de Sade set the snifter on the small table of the same wood as the paneling that was conveniently next to where she chose to sit. *"Hey wait let me get dressed up then I'll meet you on the corner we can stop along the way."* She pulled a ledger into her lap and opened it to a random page. *"To drink 'em down we gotta do this town."* Her thin brows pulled down as she began to read while the discordant jazz music surrounded her. *"Forget the name of streets as we stumble around. I won't remember your name after leavin' your bed, but I can promise ya darlin' that I'll leave while you're still cryin'."*

A quiet knock came to the door to the Captain's quarters, and Alex called out without looking up from the ledger. "Come." This was no surprise. She had requested his presence after all, so she saw no reason why she should have to open the door herself. Nigel entered with a guarded smile on his face, but it pulled to the side as his brows lifted when he heard the lyrics.

"Get her drunk as a skunk. Get her flyin' to the moon. Got her forced to the ground. She'll be traumatized soon. Well back in my day we never acted this way."

He chuckled quietly as he shut the door. "Not entirely a pleasant concept for as upbeat as the melody presents itself." He approached Alex with his hands clasped loosely behind his back. At her gesture, he sat in the chair that perfectly matched her burgundy stained leather chaise.

"I believe that is the point," she said absently since she still hadn't taken her eyes from the ledger.

Alex wasn't interested in discussing her musical tastes. She was used to being looked at oddly when it was discovered that she preferred dodgy jazz and vaudeville music to anything else. There were reasons her predilections were the way they were, but very few knew them and she was not inclined to share. Besides, the four ledgers that Geri and Laurence had brought back with them were why she had summoned her Historian to her quarters.

"Have you read through these?" The other three rested on top of each other on the low coffee table set within comfortable reach of where they sat. Nigel had initial possession of the ledgers before he sent them to her via Dr. Hennessey when the Doctor had gone to inspect the wound in her side.

Nigel had had ample time to look through them. Laurence had shifted them to Milan two days behind their present time in an effort to shake any Naviwerks interest. The Horotech had promised to look into the equipment that laid down the chrono-marker so that it would actually do what Captain Alex wanted it to do. She had no doubt that Laurence would make it work; his engineering genius was precisely why she had hired him. Meanwhile, she had disembarked to fulfill the contract, delivered the model of da Vinci's Gran Cavallo to the Castello Sforza, and received a tidy sum for her troubles. Now they were comfortably berthed in the warehouse, where she could try to make heads or tails of what filled these pages while Geri and Angel were out on a supply run.

Nigel nodded as he laced his fingers around one knee, one leg crossed casually over the other. "I have."

He almost seemed disgusted. "If what conclusions I have come to are true, those ledgers are very disturbing."

"Indeed," Alex said succinctly. She let out a breath as she set the ledger aside and finally looked at Nigel. Regret was in her impossibly light blue eyes, and she made no effort to hide it. "Nigel, I am truly sorry for the incident between us in the Mess hall. I know your feelings on the matter of your family, and I do sympathize. Forgive me for reminding you of them."

A gentle smile came to Nigel's face before he lowered his foot to the floor. He reached over to place a hand that was just as graceful and delicate as hers, only larger, onto her arm. "My dear Captain, things said between friends in the heat of emotions need not be remembered. There is nothing to forgive."

Alex smiled as her eyes lowered contritely. "You are kind to say so." She felt she owed him an apology and felt better for having offered it, even if he said it hadn't been necessary.

"However," Nigel's normal cheek entered his tone of voice. It made Alex lift her eyes to him again, and she saw the rakish smirk curl his lips. "A glass of that cognac would go a long way to eliminating the moment from my memory."

She chuckled as she gestured towards the multi-tiered, teak mini bar across from them. "Get it yourself, rogue."

Nigel caught her hand and brought it to his lips as he stood up. He pressed a light kiss to her knuckles, then he was away for the drink before she could swat him. He poured out a measure into another crystal snifter from a matching decanter. "I can't help thinking of Nash, however." He made certain that his empathy and hesitation was in his voice. When he turned back around he caught the fleeting look of hurt on Captain Alex's face. "The man bears no resemblance to the young Agent I met all those years ago. The one who won your heart."

Alex's brows creased downward into a frown more to control her emotions than any sort of resentment towards Nigel. She could not allow herself to feel anything towards Eldon anymore. What they had was gone. Anything she felt towards him now could only be used against her, and she was not the type of person to hand someone a weapon.

She knew Nigel wouldn't be put off. Honestly, she felt lucky it was he that was bringing it up, and not Dr. Hennessey. At least Nigel wouldn't press too much, nor did he know her well enough to say exactly the right thing to break down her barriers. It only benefited her to give a little then move the conversation along.

"No, he doesn't," she said in a quiet but flat tone. She picked up her glass and looked at the amber contents. "But there seems very little that can be done about that." She took a long drink as if to wash that fact down.

Nigel had moved back to his chair and reached over to put his hand once more on Alex's arm after he had sat down. "I know you are a very private person, sweetheart, but please understand that you aren't alone."

It was tempting to take him up on the offer if only to have someone to lean on. Just once. But there was one thing that carried Captain Alex through just about anything: her pride. All that she had accomplished she had done on her own. Her rise through the ranks within Naviwerks was by her efforts. Even this little rebellion she staged against the company started with her decision to leave. At one time, Nash had gotten her to open up just to him. Now, that was as finished as her career with Naviwerks. It hurt, and that was the lesson she was taking away from it. Nigel's intentions were good, but Alex would not risk being hurt again, even by a friend.

She looked at Nigel with a gentle smile on her face, but it didn't reach her eyes. Her hand came to rest on the one on her arm as if she were reassuring Nigel instead of the other way around. "I'll be fine. Thank you." She could tell that Nigel didn't entirely believe her, but as she predicted he simply nodded then took his hand back. Once more she was grateful that it was her Historian here instead of Dr. Hennessey. Abraham wouldn't have let her get away with that.

"I have had little time to study these." Alex leaned forward to remove the top ledger from the stack of three on the table. She wanted to turn the conversation into safer territory. Since she was dressed more casually in just her jodhpurs and a tank top, the movement showed off the curve of her hip along with a view of her chest. Such things were lost on Nigel, and Alex knew it. Had she been expecting anyone else she would have dressed more modestly if only for their comfort. Laurence never would have stopped blushing.

"What I have looked at is concerning." She looked at Nigel as she held the ledger out to him, her expression flattening into disapproval. Each ledger was bound in dark grey leather, plain of markings on the front cover but on the spine dates were listed underneath the Naviwerks logo with its stylized crimson N blended cleverly with an hourglass.

Nigel sighed as he took the book then opened it to a random page. "Indeed. What they suggest of Naviwerks' activities in the past is frankly horrifying." He ran his hand down the page as he shook his head. Alex thought he seemed torn between sadness and disgust. "Each ledger contains at least one century's worth of notable dates. Some are simply stated, historically accurate. Others have alterations which are recognizable, but listed are the original outcomes that I do not recall." He ran his hand gently over a page. "Listen. *Original: Fifth of November in the year of our Lord 1605. The Gunpowder Plot was foiled when an anonymous letter was delivered to William Parker days prior. Guy Fawkes was discovered guarding thirty-six barrels of gunpowder with the intent of blowing up the House of Lords and assassinating King James. Fawkes was tried and found guilty of treason, then executed by hanging. Alteration: The Gunpowder Plot proceeded as planned. No letter was received by William Parker, and King James was successfully assassinated along with prominent members of the House of Lords, November Fifth, 1605."*

Nigel closed the ledger and folded his hands over the cover where it sat in his lap. He looked at Captain Alex in mounting concern. "My books, the memory of my lessons in Leeds, they all tell me that the alteration is historically accurate, but this," he patted the ledger, "says otherwise. Naviwerks has been changing history."

"But why?" Captain Alex got a thoughtful frown on her face as she rubbed a finger over her upper lip. Her eyes narrowed in suspicion. "The Murdock Initiatives were put in place as assurances to the world's governments that Naviwerks would not abuse the power at their fingertips. Yet these ledgers tell us that they are breaking the very regulations they swore by. The risk they are taking is…"

"Untouchable." Nigel finished her sentence abruptly.

Alex gave him a confused frown for a moment. Nigel just took a lazy sip of the cognac while her mind worked that over. It didn't take long for her to come to the same conclusion. "These ledgers are the only proof there is of their actions. Every time they change something in the past our minds and memory, hell the entire *world* changes around us. The perfect crime."

Outrage set Alex's jaw, but annoyance got her up from where she had been reclining on the fainting couch. The ledger she had been perusing was left there as she began to pace. Nigel watched her and allowed silence to fall between them; they had done this many times before. One or the other would bring up a controversial topic, and the ensuing discussions had been known to go on for hours into the night as they debated details or points. This time however they were both on the same side of the matter that harbored consequences far worse than the results of the next election.

"They must benefit somehow from these changes," Alex said as her pacing turned her back towards

Nigel where he sat sipping the cognac. "Regardless, they cannot be allowed to continue."

Nigel tilted his head, excitement and curiosity brightening his light brown, almost amber eyes. "What did you have in mind?"

Alex came to a stop a few paces away from her Historian, with a new spring to her step, Nigel noted. When he had first entered her quarters, he had thought she seemed diminished some, more rounded of shoulder and uncertain. What she now had in mind had straightened her back and squared her shoulders. "We set right what they tampered with. Go back to those times and stop them from changing history." She pointed a finger firmly at the ledgers. "Those will provide the road map."

Nigel looked at the ledgers then turned a wary expression toward his Captain. "There are risks involved there, Alexandria." He paused briefly as he studied her face as if looking for something. "Meddling with time too much could…well, I don't precisely know what would happen but…"

"It can't be worse than what damage they have already caused." Alex's eyes were sharp with her conviction as she lifted her chin. Geri had told her there had been dozens of ledgers in that wing of the Vatican Library. They had no way of knowing how much history Naviwerks had already changed, but she assumed, based on her experience with the corporation, that set of ledgers was not the only set of records. No doubt the company had files stashed elsewhere. She made a mental note to find them. "At the very least we know some of what they haven't hit yet, and can police those times.

We *will* stop them, Nigel. Come Hell or high water."

Nigel let out with a resigned breath before taking a drink. After, he lifted his brows at Alex. "It will be expensive."

A sly grin formed on Alex's face as she retook her seat on the couch where she leaned on the arm towards Nigel. To the ignorant, it might look as if she were flirting with him when the reality was she was feeling smug. "So we hit them where it hurts."

Nigel's brows lifted high on his forehead as he looked at her. "What do you mean?"

"I mean, my dear Mr. Wellington," she began as she picked up her snifter again with an exaggerated and languid gesture. "Instead of giving them competition we come about. Waylay their dispatches. Scuttle their ships and take their swag." Her own slender brows lifted as she took a drink. It might be that she was feeling cheeky enough to mock Nigel's expression.

It didn't matter to him if she was. He liked the idea and smirked as he lifted his glass towards Alex. "Become pirates in fact?"

Captain Alex chuckled quietly as she touched her glass to Nigel's with a quiet clink of crystal. "Aye, matey."

Thus begins the adventures of Captain Alex and the crew of *The William's Hunt*! This probably left you with more questions than were answered, but worry not, much more is planned for our merry band of chrono-pirates. Want to know more about Agent Nash and his relationship with Captain Alex? How about a closer look into Naviwerks? Maybe you would like to know how much history is between Dr. Hennessey and Captain Alex? You can expect those answers to be addressed in the next set of episodes, but it cannot be promised that more questions will not be raised.

The story will continue with The Gunpowder Plot!

For more information on the author, upcoming appearances and episode release dates, procuring a signed copy of this book please feel free to drop by any of the following:

FaceBook: @kristacaggauthor
Instagram: @kirstacagg_author
TikTok: @kristacagg

Ain't No Way to Treat a Lady

She walked into the crowded bar alone, and made for the only two barstools left available, conveniently next to each other. The black linen dress with the thin straps looked a little worn around the edges, especially the dulled and scuffed dark blue sequins. She wore it as if it were the best thing out of her wardrobe. On another woman it might have been filled out a bit more in the places a man would notice. On her it looked like an after-thought.

She wasn't exactly unattractive. The years had been kind, but it was obvious that she had to put a little extra work into appearing the way she liked. Shoulder length straight auburn hair was duller than others. Mascara and other enhancements were required to bring out a shine in her eyes. But the faint lines at the edges of her lips suggested a ready smile hiding in there somewhere. All together, this woman was someone a man in his right mind would want to talk to, get to know.

A man like me.

Who am I? I'm Geri Reynolds. Grunt of the Naviwerks Security Corp. I'm on a night's leave. Thought I'd take in the sights and drink at my favorite watering hole. Enjoy a fine cigar. Relax. Didn't expect my preferred haunt to be filled to capacity, and definitely not with the clientele they were entertaining. Damn company made money off of renting out the docks to tours, rich folk who want to host a private party among the chrono-ships, what have you. I'd seen this place go from a hole in the wall with sawdust on the floor to bright light glaring off the copper and brass dispensers behind the bar. Can't say I was impressed, but I came here all the same. What can I say? The bartenders know me.

I watched the girl sit on the stool on the right, and placed her bag on the chair to the left as if she might be expecting company. A keen observer would notice the small roll of her eyes at the men beside the left barstool since they were acting like a bunch of apes, shouting and jumping around about some sporting event being broadcast on the steam screen behind the bar. The man to her right had barely given her a second glance. It seemed to suit her just fine since she had done the same to him before she spoke quietly with the bartender. I approved more and more.

Two minutes later a bottle of good beer was placed in front of her with no accompanying frosted glass. That impressed me. She was discerning enough to want more than just any old brew, but not so much on her dignity to not drink straight from the bottle. She had grace, but was by no means delicate as was proven when she began to eat the soup the bartender brought a few minutes later. She tucked in like a person would instead of some doll that was afraid to get smudged. After a couple of bites of soup and a drink or two of beer she pulled out a travel library panel and began to read, tuning out the rest of the patrons in the bar.

The game on the screen ended, and the bartender turned off the steam projector in an effort to encourage the rowdy boys on their way. They took the hint, and argued with each other loudly over which team played better as they left the bar. The woman had barely noticed for being lost in whatever story she was engrossed in on the panel in her hand.

Not long after the apes had left, another man joined the one on her right. Both were dandies, dressed casually but in the height of fashion with more styling products in their hair than the woman sitting quietly to their left. Their smiles were too big and too bright, and anyone in the know could tell that they had adjustments made to their eyes. The colors were just too vivid. Yin and yang, one was blonde, the other dark haired, and both had that air about them that proclaimed *I am important* to anyone looking at them. They screamed trouble, and I started paying closer attention.

The bartender didn't seem that impressed either when he stopped to take their order. I smirked as I watched him add too much water to their bourbons by "accidentally" holding the water lever of the copper dispenser for too long. The drinks were set before the gentlemen, and the bartender was gone down the bar to other customers as if they stank or something.

The dark hair was standing wedged between

the blonde and the woman. The arrogant prick actually leaned on her more than once. It finally pulled her attention out of her reader, and she gently tapped the dark haired dandy on the shoulder. A few words I couldn't catch were exchanged. She smiled as she shook her head then began to maneuver herself to the barstool to the left. Dark hair flashed her a blinding smile as he held her chair, but he only got a confused and suspicious look from her for his efforts. With a bit of pink to her cheeks she settled onto the barstool then went back to her reading as the dark hair took a seat of his own in the stool she had vacated for him.

The crowd began to thicken on that side of the bar. Richer folk with their clockwork monkeys perched on their shoulders that clicked and squeaked as if alive and wanting attention. Jointed exo-gloves encasing their fingers that did nothing more than look pretty, caught on clothing or hair and clicked against the glasses in their hands. Hydraulic heels in patent leather shoes that raised or lowered a person as they needed. They all stopped and spoke with the dandies in flowery talk and laughter that was too enthusiastic to be genuine.

The woman became distracted from her reading, and kept casting covert glances at the men beside her with a guarded curiosity shining in eyes that peered over the specs she had perched on the edge of her nose. I could have told her who they were, but I didn't want to lose my table or get involved unless I had to. Besides, someone must have dropped a name she recognized because her brows lifted, and her cheeks went pink again as she looked at the beer bottle in front of her.

During a moment between sycophants she gently placed her hand on the shoulder of the dark haired dandy. I could barely catch what she said.

"I'm sorry if I was in the way. Can I buy you both a drink to make up for it?" She had a strong voice, confident but not arrogant. Her smile was shy but honest.

Frick and Frack exchanged a cold, knowing smirk before the dark hair gave her a patronizing smile and patted her hand. "No." He beckoned the bartender over. "But we can buy you one." He waggled a finger at the beer before the woman then openly dismissed her by turning his back on her.

She looked stunned. The bartender gave her a kind smile then set a new beer in front of her which she eyed as if it had worms wriggling around in it. She turned a disgusted look to the dark hair's back, shook her head with another roll of her eyes then picked up the beer for a long drink.

Not long after, the bartender returned to the gentlemen, and placed a couple of chits in front of each of them. The dandies looked at the chits then to the bartender who jerked his head towards the other end of the bar. "Compliments of the ladies down the way."

The blonde looked down the bar where a flock of giggles stood with empty smiles and shorter frocks that looked fresh from the seamstress. "Now that's more like it, mate," he said to his partner with a grin.

As they laughed, the woman gave them a glare then signaled the bartender who came to stand before her with a tight smile on his face. She gave him a similar smile. "I believe I'll settle up, thank you. I've had all of the atmosphere I can take." She handed the bartender enough money to cover her tab then gathered her bag.

The dandies heard her. Would have been hard to miss since I caught it from where I sat, but instead of being insulted they looked smug. The bastards.

They didn't say a word as she walked past them. She wasn't comfortable by any stretch of the imagination. That much was obvious by the set of her jaw. The laughter that filled the air from the fops before she was out of earshot, and the twittering noises from the frocks at the corner of the bar didn't do nothing more than stiffen her shoulders, but I could tell her dinner had been ruined.

I watched it all from where I sat in the corner with my boots on the table, and an unlit cigar in the corner of my mouth. I saw the look on her face as she left. Offended, disappointed with an edge of sadness. Ain't a reason in the world a woman should wear an expression like that, and I turned my attention back solidly on the culprits that put it there.

I had recognized them long before she had. Hard not to when you couldn't walk down the docks without having to dodge the riggings and ticker tape cameras set up all over for whatever those two were filming now. Wasn't the first time the movie shoot had irritated me. Now I was downright fed up. I waited.

Hours later the bartender was finally shooing the dandies from the bar. The frocks had already left when it became obvious that the gentlemen weren't going to do more than accept the chits they sent, and drink themselves stupid on their nickel. I had settled up with the waitress long ago, and she'd already gone home with a smile for the generous tips she'd gotten from me. I had also sent a little something to the bar to keep the bartenders from so much as looking at me. As I got up to follow the meandering dandies out the door I tipped an invisible hat to one of them who smirked back at me in appreciation. It always helped to be a recognized regular.

Being as late as it was, the streets were empty and quiet except for the two chuckleheads who failed to realize that they no longer had to talk over a crowd to be heard. The cobblestones were slick from the humidity in the air. Occasionally, a blonde or dark head would bob from dress shoes slipping out from under the weight of an inflated ego. It was a straight shot down the street to the warm and comfortable wagons the "noble" celebrities were staying in while they were on location, but they still turned down a side street. I knew where that one ended, and turned down a small lane to cut them off.

They came laughing around a corner, hanging on to each other and dickering about which way the wagons were. It didn't take much effort to step out from a stack of crates behind them, and knock their heads together. They were so far gone that their skulls connecting put their lights out, and dropped them there in the lane. Puddles of stagnant water that contained all manner of substances best not thought about seeped into those fine, tailor made clothes. It was a temptation to turn their faces so they woke up with a mouth full of the foul stuff.

The yellow light of a struck match lit up my frowning face. White-blue smoke puffed out into the sticky night as I lit the stub of the cigar I'd kept hold of. I had to get back to the ship. The Captain would be waiting on me before we pushed on to our next swag grab, probably some necklace an old matron lost seven years gone, and couldn't live without. But I couldn't resist teaching these two bounders a lesson.

Blowing out a plume of smoke, I looked down at the unconscious gentlemen, and pulled out a fat marker I used to write on stock crates. I crouched down next to them, and worked the permanent ink onto their skin. I smirked when I stood up, admiring my handiwork.

"Ain't no way to treat a lady, boys," I grumbled, then turned to walk out the way the two drunkards had come in.

Dollymop was spelled out in clear, bold letters on the cheek of the dark hair, while *Molly* was written on the forehead of his fellow. I wore a satisfied grin for a day straight. A personal record.

About the Author

Krista has come full circle in her life. Born and raised in a small town in Pennsylvania, she moved to Savannah, GA after she graduated from art school in New Jersey. From there she moved to Olympia, WA…then back to Savannah, and ultimately back to Pennsylvania. She lives near her father with her husband and four furry demons (cats). For fun, she cultivates her squirrel army in the backyard.

As an active pagan for many decades, Krista has come to understand that there is more to our natural world than meets the common senses. She lived with ghosts in Savannah. Seen things in the thick forests of the Pacific Northwest. Investigated hauntings in Pennsylvania. There may never be a time when Krista doesn't look for the undiscovered.

CPSIA information can be obtained
at www.ICGtesting.com
Printed in the USA
BVHW041914220623
666269BV00002B/11